Ninja Mommy
Maritime Magic

忍者ナニー

NATALIE NEWPORT

SYNCLECTIC MEDIA

Copyright © 2013 by Natalie Newport

Published by **Synclectic Media**
Seattle, Washington
www.synclectic.com

Publisher's Cataloging-in-Publication Data

Newport, Natalie
  Ninja Mommy / Natalie Newport. – 1st ed.
    p. cm. –
  Summary: In the sequel to Ninja Nanny, our superheroine Natalie Newport is faced with new challenges: to refine her superpowers (including being a new mommy) and to conquer the high seas! She reunites with a few old friends, makes new acquaintances, and battles an evil ninja wizard—all during her quest to reunite with a long lost loved one. During her travels, Natalie navigates her way to the most valuable treasures she has ever known.
  Book two of the Ninja Nanny series
  Library of Congress Control Number: 2013934622
  ISBN: 978-0615781037
    [1. Action & Adventure—Fiction. 2. Romance—Fiction. 3. Coming of Age—Fiction.] I. Title.
PS3613.E97   2013934622
[Fic]—813.6N   P-CIP

---

10 9 8 7 6 5 4 3 2 1

Ω
Book Two of the Ninja Nanny Series

First Edition
Printed in the United States

Dedicated to:

My mom, who was my lighthouse.

Thanks to:

My wonderful friends and family, who have been endlessly
supportive of my writing.

Copy Editor Jim Thomsen: Desolation Island Editing
Services; thomsen1965@gmail.com for the wonderful and
timely editing.

Part One

*The sea,
once it casts its spell,
holds one in its net of wonder
forever.*

Jacques Eves Cousteau

Introduction

"The ocean," he said. "It's the most powerful force in the world."

We had just arrived, spontaneously, and stood side by side gazing out at it. He turned to face me, and I him.

"Study it, the way it ebbs and flows, how it breathes, softly in and out. It draws in its breath, building up and exhaling its force. Always expanding and retracting, giving and taking, flowing.

Study this; the way it keeps moving despite what's going on in the world. Thank it for its life-giving nutrients. Use it for cleansing purposes. Give back to it by picking pollutants out whenever you see them. Serenade and worship water, for it is your element."

Jin hadn't spoken any of these words. He simply infused his knowledge into me with one soft touch of his fingers to my temple.

We stood in the warm sand at the ancient Place of Refuge on the Big Island of Hawaii in the morning sunlight. He barely touched my hand, and instantly we were transported to a tide pool. He knelt down so I followed suit.

"Feel the energy of the lava," he said, touching a large formation beside him. I touched it, sensing the ancient wisdom of observation within—how it had solidified from hot, molten lava into its current statuesque shape beside the sea.

"And of the coral," he continued, picking up a small white piece and handing it to me. I touched it and instantly knew its life history. I saw what it had seen, felt what it had felt. The tide pool teemed with life: all kinds of fish, crabs and crustaceans swam and scuttled around, all doing their jobs in their tiny community.

I honed in with laser-like vision, down to the microscopic minutiae. The ocean was filled with so much life, most of which we couldn't see. I was able to feel the pulse of the planet through it.

We touched the sand and felt its vibration. "All things have their own vibration, Natalie," he said. "You can tune in when you need to ground and center, to unify with the earth. It's available for you when you need it. Trust me, you will."

"I do trust you, Sifu. Implicitly," I replied.

He seemed to be trying to convey something that I wasn't getting, so I searched his face for clues. Noting my quizzical expression, Jin answered with a look of deep worry and fear that I had never seen on his face before. "There is danger in our midst. We must be very aware of our surroundings from this point on," he warned.

I felt the energy of fear and anger pouring out of him. He snapped out of it, took a deep breath and told me not to dwell on it, to just be very alert. "I will," I agreed, a shiver making its way down my spine at the possibility of what was to come, and tried to shake off the feeling.

We stood up and I bowed to him in a formal gesture of thanks for his latest lesson. He took my hands in his, a tiny smile playing on his lips. "We're off," he said, and indeed we were, the waves erasing our footprints, as if we'd never been. I knew from that point on my life would never be the same.

~*~

Jin was my martial arts trainer and mentor. He had trained me for several years now, and had seen me through some important events in my life. Actually, he had always been there, ever since I was born. I just didn't always know it. He made an appearance during my childhood and then had come fully into my life in my late teens to train me in Jeet Kune Do and other forms, advancing me rapidly.

And then through Jin's guidance and quite possibly some divine guidance as well, I had been informed that I was a superheroine in training. I was to be a super ninja of sorts. This means in addition to defying gravity within the realm of martial arts, I had actual real superpowers, such as teleportation and resistance to heat. (I was told there might be more, but I wasn't sure what they might be yet).

It took me a while to get used to these, but after I did, boy did I work it! I could use them only for the highest good…and if this meant getting to and from my destination more quickly, so be it. That was allowed, and this got me excited about my new identity.

I also had a new life. Jin had been an ear for me while I figured out my feelings for this firefighter known as Hammer, the love of my life. In martial arts, and Buddhism, non-attachment is key. Not getting attached helps limit or omit pain…except when it comes to love. Love kind of throws the status quo out of whack, but at the same time it restores balance to the universe.

Jin and his female counterpart, Jade, my mentor of sorts, helped me wrap my mind around that concept. As an independent type, I came to see that I could and did need someone in my life, in the romantic sense.

Well, the firefighter and I were now married. He knew about my superhero status, and didn't mind it a bit. He was contemporary like that.

I had a best friend, Sam, who I'd gone on a road trip with last year. I figured things out on that trip too. Sometimes it takes being away from home to be able to see clearly; a bit of distance and perspective can work wonders. She and I were close, but she'd moved away to California after getting together with a firefighter we met on our road trip, so I missed her like whoa these days.

But life was good. Martial arts and daily yoga helped me release tension and focus on learning. I needed that, because being a superhero in a small town was not easy to keep under wraps, and I didn't want the drama of the paparazzi outside my door!

*Only when the clamor of the outside world
is silenced will you be able to
hear the deeper vibration.
Listen carefully.*

Sarah Ban Breathnach

Chapter 1

"Can't do it!" Cameron, one of my two cantankerous charges, shouted from atop the stairs. *"CAAAAAN'T DOOO IIIIIT!!!"*

I told him I'd be right up to help. He was trying to do the zipper on his pants so he could use the bathroom, but I was having tummy problems from drinking too much coffee and couldn't make it at the moment. Good thing Courtney was still in her crib, even though she was too old for it. I couldn't handle having her watch me on the toilet. I had gotten caught in traffic today on the way to the house, and that meant the father—or the male C as I referred to him because the family's last name started with C—would miss his ferry and my ass would be fired.

"CAN'T DO IT!" Cameron was bellowing now. My stomach churned. His voice started to quiver. Now he was crying. Screaming and wailing that he couldn't do it. *Never intentionally raise a perfectionist*, I thought. *Far too much work.* "Can't…DO…it," he screeched through tears. By the time I got to the top of the stairs, he was red-faced, hands with a death grip on his pants where he had tried to button them. The zipper was stuck, too. *Buy a copy of "Don't Sweat the Small Stuff" and replace his naptime story with it*, I thought.

Just as I reached for him, Courtney let out a bloodcurdling scream, and said that there were snakes in her crib, so Cameron and I ran into her room, and she laughed and threw a stuffed snake at my face. She just laughed and laughed and jumped up and down in her crib, thinking it was hilarious that she'd tricked us.

And then Cameron turned into the devil, and Courtney into a flying gargoyle type of creature, and they came after me. I tried to disappear. "We still see you, Natalie!" they whispered in unison, with the same tone of the sisters in *The Shining*. I ran out the door and tripped over a real snake, because by now there were tons of them, coiled up in piles around the yard outside, hissing, rattling, and slithering. I tried to navigate my way out of this snake maze, and then for some reason they all slithered away or into holes.

And then I saw the reason: an enormous, black and red and very pregnant Black Widow spider! This nasty monster actually made the ground vibrate as it approached. I closed my eyes and tried to teleport to anywhere but here—to no avail! It was like my legs were stuck to the ground. I couldn't run or hide.

The monstrous arachnid thundered towards me. I shielded myself with my arms, but it knocking me down, hovering over me, digestive juices dripping out of its mouth. "Aaaaaaaaaah!" I screamed as it picked me up and carried me to a darker spot, ideal for not being interrupted during its meal. The spider crouched down, moving in for the kill. Eight horrible eyeballs looked at me. I shuddered in horror at the clicking and grinding sound of the spider's jaws as the fangs came out to inject poison into my body, getting closer and closer— hot, sweaty, gross. I felt the fangs begin to pierce my skin. "Ouch!"

And then I woke up sweating.

Oh, Praise Buddha! It was just a dream. A weird, random dream about the job I used to have, the kids I used to nanny, and it had spiraled into my greatest fear: spiders. I processed for a minute, regaining my orientation. In the real world, I had already gotten canned for taking the kids—because I had no one to leave them with—to a fire I was led to believe their parents were trapped in. It was all a misunderstanding that turned into a difference of opinion about how things should be handled, and led to me seeing those parents for what they were—people who cared only how things appeared on the surface, to society.

So at least that was over. I couldn't be fired again from a job I'd already been fired from—phew! Also, I wasn't actually having diarrhea, or being eaten by a spider—bonus! I took a deep breath, sighing in relief, and looked over to see if I'd woken Hammer up. He wasn't there. Damn. And then I heard singing, coming from the bathroom. Not Hammer. He didn't sing. Ever. Plus this was a female voice. I sat bolt upright in bed, frozen in place, straining to hear.

"Just another manic Monday, whoa oh ooh whoa
Wish it was Sunday
That's my fun day, whoa oh ooh whoa
My I don't have to run dayeeee…"

Whoever this was had a lovely singing voice, but it was not The Bangles in my bathroom. The singing made it unlikely that its voice belonged to an axe murderer. Maybe it was just a friendly singing ghost, right? So I slunk out of bed and crept to the door on silent feet.

"Six o'clock already
I was just in the middle of a dream.
I was kissing Valentino by a crystal blue Italian stream…"

Right around "Valentino," I nudged the door open, and caught Kiki standing on her back two legs, front two clasped in front of her holding my toothbrush and singing in front of the mirror. I stifled a gasp, and then a giggle, and then saw Claw behind her, Hammer's toothbrush in his paws.

"Oh no I can't be late," she continued. "Oh no," Claw sang backup. He was an alto.

"Cause then I guess I just won't get paid. These are the days when you wish your bed was already made."

I could not believe my eyes or ears. I not only had talking cats, but singing ones. My eyes watered as I stood in silent gales of laughter. Kiki praised Claw for being on key and on time this time, and Claw sighed, sounding like he totally didn't want to be doing this.

I laughed again, but then had what I thought was a dizzy spell. Suddenly, I was sucked out of the room and sat facing my trainer in the garden behind the pagoda.

"Phoenix. Welcome."

"Thanks. Did you call me here?"

"I summoned you.

"Out of my crazy dream?"

"It would seem so, yes."

"I hear it's just another manic Monday," I said. He belly-laughed—one of the few times I'd ever heard him do that.

"Wow, this is a first," I said, still tripping on what'd just happened. "A vision within a dream within a dream, about a cat singing a song about a dream." I rubbed my eyes. It was all too much.

"More of a visit than a vision," he corrected. "And perhaps a premonition in there too," he said. I wondered if I was by chance still dreaming. Sifu didn't usually just sit and laugh this way. He chuckled. "Nope, you're awake now."

"Well since I'm here…why am I here?" I asked, half smiling, hoping we weren't going to train in the middle of the night.

"Oh, come now, Phoenix, you know I like to work you hard, but I would never train with you in the middle of the night. I believe in sleep just as much as you do.

"Can I get that in writing?"

Jin chortled. "The reason I called you was, I got the feeling your dreams were causing you some stress. And we can't have that on Ninja Nanny's birthday, now, can we?"

"What? It's my…?" With so much going on, I had completely spaced my birthday!

Jin shook his head. "Tsk-tsk. Not allowed to forget your birthday. That breaks so many rules of the universe, I can't even begin to tell you."

"Uh oh."

"Yep," he said, twinkle in his eye. "I may have to get Jade involved in deciding your punishment for breaking the rules."

Jade appeared, smiling, holding a white-frosted cake with a single candle in it. "It's a sugar-free, fat-free recipe. Even the frosting," she said. "I know that's the only way you'll eat cake." I grinned at her. Jin and Jade were experts at reading my mind, and my life. I hoped it was chocolate under there.

"Of course," Jade said.

It was a bit unnerving sometimes, the way they knew what I was thinking, but I had learned to love it. Saved me from asking a *lot* of questions.

"Happy birthday, Phoenix."

"Thank you." I smiled, teared up a little, made a wish, and blew out my candle.

"This year of your life will be filled with challenges," Jin said. "All you have to do is believe, and you will achieve."

I noticed that massage therapist/health guru Colin was there too. He wished me a happy birthday, and immediately gave me a neck massage as I sat, taking the occasional bite of cake. I felt myself fading into sleep again.

This time, I woke up and wondered if I was really awake. Maybe Hammer could help me validate my waking state, I thought with a smile, because I had somehow made it back to my own bed in my own house. I reached over and discovered, again, that he wasn't there. Sigh. The sun hadn't yet shown itself, which meant Hammer was working a local fire, or away fighting a more remote forest blaze. I'd become an expert at sleeping through these things, but that bothered me. I never wanted him to leave without saying goodbye. Every time he left could very well be the last time I saw him. Firefighting was sketchy like that. And Hammer meant the world to me.

So did the little mini me/mini Hammer that I had just given birth to, which was part of the reason he didn't want to wake me. I'd given birth a little over six months ago and was still recovering. Hammer's mom had spoiled me. She didn't know I was a secret ninja-in-training, and Hammer and I were keeping that fact under wraps for now.

I had worried long and hard over what to do when I found out I was pregnant. I wasn't sure how it happened. I mean, I know *how* it happened, but we had used protection *every time*. So apparently this little sprout really wanted through. I didn't know if I was ready for a child. It seemed a lot to take on, especially since I'd recently found out I was a superhero, and hadn't yet earned my wings, so to speak.

The best way out is always through, I've been told. Not that I wanted out. I just wanted to know how I was going to balance being a wife, mother, and a ninja-in-training all at once.

The wife part I had down. The mothering would require help, which Hammer's mother would be giving, along with some of Sam's friends from the bank. Plus I had a stack of books on my nightstand all about how to care for a new baby that had replaced the "what to do during your pregnancy" ones. I was making my way through them and almost finished. I had almost no time to read between changing diapers, working, training, and the million other things I did each day, but usually snuck in twenty minutes at the end of the day. It helped me unwind.

I got up, splashed some water on my face, and thought about the next day. I would go to work at seven a.m. when my morning babysitter got here. As much as I craved sleep these days, I found it nice to get up while most people were still asleep, and greet the day. The air seemed fresher, there was less traffic, and as long as I went to bed early enough, I was chipper. I would never be a morning person, but I wasn't grumpy either—just happy to be alive, and providing people's caffeine.

I still worked at the coffee shop near the fire station. When Hammer was around, he would pick me up when my shift ended. This of course was just for show, as I had, a little over nine months ago, found out I could disappear and reappear in another location—all part of being a superhero-in-training. Hammer and I would go out to lunch, or work out together—this reminded us of how we met, and kept our relationship like new. Though not without its challenges, this was a sweet life.

I didn't have to work, but I felt the need to help out with the bills, and socialize with fellow coffee lovers. When I was pregnant, the hardest part was not being allowed to drink as much coffee, but still having to work around it and smell the beautiful aroma. Those days were over. I had birthed not one but two babies: Andrew Makai, and Zoe Mer. Both of their middle names related to the ocean because that's where I first got a cramp that led to discovering the pregnancy. Makai means "sea" in Hawaiian, and Mer is the French. At first, I was just plain scared, but now, I couldn't be more thrilled. The feeling I got when I found out over the phone that I was with child was enough to change my mind. Luckily, Hammer concurred.

They both had Hammer's deep blue eyes—so beautiful, almost aquamarine looking. I loved the baby smell and the feel of their skin. Many times when I took them for walks in the double wide stroller, I talked to them and felt like they could understand me.

Life wasn't all wine and roses by any means. My being pregnant had made Hammer and I both irritable at times. Like the time when we'd fought about conserving water. He told me to conserve it because the firefighters needed as much as possible.

"Well, what about the planet?" I asked.

"The firefighters and fire victims are part of the planet and you should conserve water with everyone in mind, but especially them."

I didn't like being lectured, especially when my back hurt, feet were swollen, and I had to pee every fecking five minutes. My baths were much needed. I didn't even fill them up that much because I was such a tub that my body weight filled up the tub I was in! So I didn't think the lecture was necessary.

"Well, what about Micronesian children with not enough food or water? They are just as important." It was just about then that we both started laughing at our ridiculous argument. We never fought about typical things like who did which chores or anything, just asinine things. We looked at the world differently. But that's what made it exciting, and endlessly interesting.

I told him I'd kick his butt—figuratively speaking of course—if he referred to us, as a couple, as being pregnant. That was trendy and progressive of men to do, but until they had to carry the child, or children, as it were, to term by taking on four-point-five of those nine long months, it was *me* who was pregnant. He didn't have a problem with that. In fact, he had his own reasons for not wanting to, one of which I quickly deduced was that the guys in the department would never let him hear the end of it. They all had good hearts, but they were not exactly progressives in the gender wars. Their focus was, and rightly so, on saving lives, forests, and buildings.

I had the babies in water at the hospital, and that was one time Hammer didn't say a word about the use of water. Ever since I'd considered being a mother, I'd thought of doing it that way. It just seemed like such a natural way to go about it, more comfortable for the babies to come out swimming. Plus, it was symbolic because of Hammer's chosen profession. I hoped they would always be safe from fire.

When my wonderful husband was home working with the local department, we'd spend some quality time together, Hammer would go back to work, and most days I would spend some time at the gym and work out with Sifu. The kids could go into daycare there while I did that.

I had trained intensively for three years in Jeet Kune Do and other martial arts forms that are so covert I can't even tell you about them. My newest challenge was the most interesting one to date: Operation Ninja. It was *ON*.

I was pretty sure my teacher was having a hard time with me. I was a tough student, wanting to know the reason for everything. Why do I have to throw the Ninja star like *this*, when it feels more natural this *other* way? Why do I have to move my back foot to the four o'clock position when I do such and such a maneuver? Knowing why helped me remember things. If I knew why I had to do it, it made sense. I was a logical ninja-in-training. This was probably the only area of life in which I was naturally logical, so it worked. I was good at martial arts.

Jin was great at explaining why, and very patient. For example, he explained that I had to move my back foot to four o'clock so my attacker couldn't get me if he punched straight out. From that angle, I was protected. Brilliant. I loved training.

*It's not how much we give
but how much love
we put into giving.*

Mother Teresa

Chapter 2

I got home, put my keys on the hook that my oh-so-logical-in-every-possible-way Virgo firefighter husband had installed, and closed my eyes, hoping for a 5-minute power nap since Hammer was home and watching the kids. The TV was on and the news about missing kids was blaring, so I couldn't help opening my eyes again. So many had gone missing in the US in the last year, it was truly tragic. There were none missing from our area from this latest string of disappearances which the authorities felt was related, but it seemed to be moving across the country from East to West—but going unnaturally fast. Virginia. Pennsylvania. New York. Missouri. Nebraska. The footage of sobbing parents really got me in the heart. Hammer came in and I asked if he'd seen this story. He said no, and sat down to watch with me, as riveted as I was by this crime committed by a thief who had left no clues.

Finally, Hammer gave me a kiss on the top of the head from behind the couch and said he was going to bed. I wanted to watch the whole story so I told him I'd join him in a few minutes.

I must have fallen asleep there, because when I opened my eyes, Kiki and Claw were on my chest, looking at me expectantly. They demanded love, food, and more love, in that exact order. I had no problem with any of their demands, as long as they didn't ask me for more Krispy Kremes. That'd been a one-time treat, and I only gave them each a tiny bit but they were bouncing off the walls while Hammer and I were trying to pack for our trip to California. Never again. It was back to Friskies and Fancy Feast for these two. I had tried the healthier stuff, and they wouldn't touch it.

As I dished up a can each, feeling fully awake now, I heard footsteps behind me, turned around and saw a gorgeous hunk that resembled some combination of Matthew McConaughey and Joaquin Phoenix, with a little Colin Firth in there too. I still didn't know how exactly I had scored such a hottie. But I wasn't questioning it. I liked a little wildness in my men—wild, but balanced. The one I'd married was the perfect blend.

Hammer!

"Well hello there, insanely hot guy standing in the kitchen!" I said, rising to give him a hug. He hugged me back, his lips in my hair, kissing my neck.

"You never came back to bed," he pouted.

"Sorry. Fell asleep out there. Our couch is too comfortable."
"You smell amazing," he said.

"I do? Must be the baby lotion."

He smiled. "Natalie, we have to talk."

"Yes, we do. You first."

He looked at me for a minute with question marks in his eyes. "Everything's fine, but I'm thinking about coming home and returning to work for the fire department, permanently."

"But you love the trips away. Right?"

"I do. But number one, I want to be here for you and the babies. I don't want to be gone for days on end with you spending your nights alone. The truth is, I hate leaving you."

"And I hate it when you leave. But I'm used to being alone. I've been alone for most of my life, so if that's the reason—"

"It's a large part of it. I know you can handle yourself, but before long there will be two crawling toddlers in the house. Plus, the money is better with the local department. I wouldn't have to be gone for as long. Local fires are contained, forest fires are endless."

"I know. As well as dangerous, as evidenced by what happened in Arizona—I'm so relieved that you weren't there. I always worry when you leave on these trips."

"Well then, that settles it."

"Really? I mean, really for real?"

"Yes!"

"Ohhh!" I tackled him and covered him with kisses. He laughed. "The guys will be so happy to have you back."

"Yeah, I thought about that. Especially Tim. I've missed them all so much."

"I know you have. When you're gone they call me once a week to check on me, and find out how you're doing."

"Really? I had no idea." He thought about that for a second, blinking away tears. The brotherhood ran deep, and while Hammer had been away, it was like having a big extended family looking after me. "They're really good guys."

"They are."

"Another thing is, on those trips we always have to wait around to be pulled in. We go hungry as often there isn't quite enough food to feed everyone. We're starving and sweaty for hours. And the showers suck."

"Oh, the agony!"

"Indeed."

"I'm so happy you've chosen this, Hammer. You tried it, you found out it wasn't exactly for you, but at least you'll never wonder what could've been." This put a satisfied smile on his face. I couldn't have been more proud of him.

"So what's new with you, ninja-in-training?"

I laughed. "Training is going very well. I've had some adventures I'll have to tell you about soon, but you'll have to keep them a secret."

"I can do that."

"What else, what else…oh! I got an interesting phone call yesterday."

"Really? From?"

"The family I used to nanny for. The C's."

"Oh, yeah?" His voice grew more interested.

"They want me back. They fired my replacement because they found drugs in her room. Apparently, she was involved with not only weed but meth, among other things, and she left the tools out in the open, didn't even try to hide them."

"Oh, no."

"Yep. I thought she just smoked a little herb to relax now and again, but that wasn't the case. She was involved in selling, too. All of it."

"Now that's a *real* reason to fire a nanny," he said. He'd been so angry about their reason for firing me, and I knew he still felt guilty because he hadn't had time to take us all back to my apartment the night of the movie theater fire, when Cameron had snuck into the fire engine and we'd all had to follow. "What did you tell them?"

"I actually said I'd think about it. I wanted to get your thoughts on the subject."

"Well, I know you miss Cameron and Courtney."

"That I do. Plus I don't think they get enough love from their parents. Just a lot of discipline designed to mold them into perfect children."

"Which we know don't exist."

"Exactly. And, the money is good." Unfortunately, being a ninja didn't pay other than in karma. "Better than espresso, even with the tips I make."

"So I say, do what you want. In the end, it's up to you."

"Yes. I told them no, not half an hour ago."

He rubbed his hands over his face, which he did when he was relieved. "I was so hoping you'd say that. I didn't want you to go back to working for those parents. They just don't deserve you."

"Yeah, I just don't think it'd work out. What happened between us, and how they judged me for my actions…"

"Precisely."

"But, I don't want to do coffee forever."

"I understand. But the stress level is pretty low for you, right? As compared to being a nanny?"

"Yes. And right now I need as little stress as possible, so I can focus on training our future badasses." Hammer smiled and put his hand on my stomach.

"Nice and flat already."

"There's still a little pooch, but I don't mind," I said. It reminded me that I was a mother now, in addition to being a major international sex symbol. ☺

"Have you been dreaming lately?"

"Yeah, a little…" I lied, not wanting him to worry about me.

"I thought so. You talk in your sleep a lot, Miss."

"Really? Anything interesting?"

"Mostly nonsense. Although I have picked up a few tidbits about being a Mom, and some definite pointers on how to throw a Ninja star…"

I play-punched him in the arm. "Didn't anyone teach you it's impolite to listen in?"

"It's kind of hard when your mouth is up against my ear," he countered.

"Sorry." He could still make me blush.

"It's okay. I like it. It makes me laugh."

"And disturbs your sleep."

"Hey, it's good training now that I'll be home more often to be awakened by our offspring," he said softly. He looked at me with those penetrating, sparkly blue eyes and cupped my face in his hands, kissing me. That was the kiss that told me he meant business. So I snuck a peek at the kids who were sleeping comfortably. We had gotten very efficient at our us-time, assisted by the wonderful invention of baby monitors. We adjourned to the bedroom. He picked me up in one fell swoop, making me feel light and feminine—not an easy feat, considering I'm a pretty buff chick who had just had twins, but easy for Hammer. He carried me into our room, and I realized just how much I'd missed him.

~*~

I awoke while it was still dark outside, and looked over at the clock. Four a.m. sharp. I wasn't sure what'd woken me up. No singing this time. Hammer was home. I noticed a box on the nightstand, wrapped in Asian style paper with little pagodas all over it. How had Hammer snuck that in without me noticing?

Not hearing anything from the baby monitors yet and knowing I still had a few minutes before the twins stirred awake, I slipped out of bed and went into the bathroom (after doing a quick check—nope, no cats in there this time) to open it. The tiny attached card said: *To Natalia, the love of my life. To remind you that I'm always with you in spirit, even when I can't physically be with you.* Melt. I would put it in the photo album/scrapbook I'd been working on since we got married.

The box held a jewelry box. I opened it slowly, and gasped.

He'd gotten me a phoenix necklace. The silver phoenix rose from amber and amethyst fire. The gift was absolutely breathtaking, and I had never seen anything like it. I felt the heat of tears on my face, and then his arms around my waist.

"Didn't want you to think I'd forgotten. Happy birthday."

I was speechless except for a simple "thank you" through the tears. He scooped me up and carried me into the kitchen, opening the fridge and pulling something out, and then taking me back to bed. He fed me strawberries and chocolate, after which we fell fast asleep.

I've met many thinkers
and many cats,
but the wisdom of cats is
infinitely superior.

Hippolyte Taine

Chapter 3

Besides raising twins, keeping my hubby happy (which really wasn't as challenging as I thought it'd be, as he was good at keeping himself happy with projects), and training, I felt compelled to figure out my own happiness.

Hammer had decided that career firefighting was it for him, but I still didn't know what I was meant to do. I knew I wanted to work, not just be a mom and a ninja-in-training. I wanted to be *in* the world, and have grown-up conversations. I needed that, or I felt my brain would turn to mush.

"Donnnn't overthink it, Nnnatalie-mrow."

Uh oh. The cats were talking to me again!

"You're right, Kiki. You're always right."

"I knnnnow I ammmeow." Kiki replied, a bit haughtily.

"So, can you give me advice? Can you see the future, Kiki? Is that your superpower?"

"Nnno. It's Claw's. Ask him. It's time for my nnnap," she said, and sort of flounced into the bedroom.

"All this time, and you haven't told me Claw was also a stealth cat?" I said under my breath. I heard a high pitched "Harumph" from the bedroom. I loved my cat. She had such an attitude.

I turned to Claw. "Claw, have you been holding out on me?"

He chuckled. His laugh reminded me of the dog on the old Dick Dastardly cartoons, Muttley.

"Do you have any words of wisdom you'd like to share?"

"Mmmmaybe, for a small price."

"Name your price."

"First, the can of tuna that's in the cupboard. I know it's there, I saw it this morning. Very pleasing to the feline palate, you know. And second, a scratch behind the ears and under the chin."

"Done. But the tuna can be second, I don't want to smell tuna breath while we talk."

"Deal." Claw's voice sounded a bit like Professor Snape from the Harry Potter movies.

He cuddled up next to me, head-butting my hand. "So…any general words of wisdom before I get started with the questioning?"

He yawned. "Nnno."

"Okay, you've been with us a year so you know my life. Assuming you don't use the crystal ball method because I don't see one anywhere around, what should I know about it?"

"That you'rrre heading in the right dirrrrection," he said, his r's sounding like an extended purr.

"Anything else? More specific maybe?"

He put his paws over his eyes for a minute, concentrating. It was totally cute. I scratched him some more. "Ohhh, right there. Thanks. He removed his paws and looked up at me, deep into my eyes. "Natalie, your challenges will get harder, but you will not be given anything you can't handle. You're going to grow a lot in the next year. Hammer will always be okay. You will have to protect your twins, especially when Hammer isn't around to help. And I see…big surprises in store for you, young lady. *Huge*." And with that, his eyes glazed over and he closed them while I continued to scratch. I closed my eyes too, for a short time, and then started awake when he put his paw on my mouth.

"Thanks for the advice," I said, kissing his forehead. Claw had no response. He jumped up and joined Kiki in the bedroom. As he turned the corner and I got up to check on the twins, I could've sworn I saw him smiling like the Cheshire Cat from Alice in Wonderland.

"Poo, I forgot to ask about the singing," I thought to myself.

When you find your place,
practice begins.

Dogen

Chapter 4

"You can go anywhere from here, Phoenix. The *where* is up to you." I was in a field with cows in the distance. Dragonflies, butterflies and birds flitted around us. Plants rustled in the breeze. Jin put his hands on my shoulders.

"Welcome to your Zen."

"I created this?"

"Yes. You can create places of tranquility for yourself. This one, I reached in to your psyche a little and grabbed and brought us here with your vision. The places we've visited together, you can revisit, modifying them for your needs at the time. You can also create places to practice."

"And opponents?"

"Yes, but be careful with this. Start small, grasshopper." He smiled, and I had to laugh. I didn't usually hear Jin make references to pop culture, but once in a while he did, taking me by surprise. "Before," he continued, you drew whomever you needed and who was available to you for advice, help. Now, you can summon them to improve your technique and fight them if you wish. In fact, I was going to suggest it as part of your training."

"Will I know who's coming from now on?"

"Unfortunately, it's not that simple."

"Life never is."

"Indeed it isn't, Phoenix. You can try to summon the one you think will give you the best advice in the moment, but if that entity isn't available, you'll be surprised."

Big surprises, Claw had said. "Like the time Yoda showed up."

"Exactly." I saw a twinkle of humor in Jin's eyes.

"Jin, can I ask you a…logistical question?"

"Sure."

"Who will look after the kids if I go to the Pagoda, or have one of these…episodes? We have a babysitter, but…"

"That's an easy one. Me."

"Really? Taking time out from your busy schedule…"

"Is not an imposition. I love your kids as if they were my own. You and they are very close to my heart, Natalie. Hammer too, although I don't know him well formally. I've seen him, with and without you and he is a very good soul."

I was close to tears. I didn't have to ask what'd happen if Jin was busy, or with me. I knew Jade would also take care of my babies. "Yes, she will," Jin said softly. He knew exactly what I was thinking, all of the time, which was disconcerting, but oddly comforting. I hugged him.

"Furthermore, Natalie, they will need our protection." A shiver went through me as he said that. But I saw in his face that the subject wasn't open for discussion. "Now, let's get to work."

"What're we learning today, Sifu?"

"Close your eyes, and come with me," he said, taking my hands in his.

*All that we are is a result
of what we have thought.
The mind is everything.
What we think
we become.*

Buddha

Chapter 5

Jin and I reappeared inside my house. Walking through a few rooms, he eyed every detail. Before we could start, Jin said that I needed to change the energy around my house. I needed to improve my Feng Shui. Our house needed to be transformed into a sort of Zen home base, so that we could be fully functional in our jobs and lives. This also meant I needed to talk to Hammer—I was lucky, because he was off work for two days. He'd gone back to the local department already and was working twenty-four on and forty-eight off. Jin told me we'd resume training the next day.

Jin disappeared and I found Hammer in the kitchen, with our favorite Matchbox 20 playing low on the stereo so as not to disturb the kids. Hammer stood polishing the silver his parents had given us. I just stared at him, so intent on his work. He never ceased to amaze me with his projects. He smiled without looking up, sensing my presence. "I've already done some welding, cleaned and vacuumed my car, done the dishes, cleaned the cat box, and changed a couple dirty diapers." That's when he looked up to see the expression on my face, which was somewhere between shock, awe and delight. I loved how willing he was to get things done, even clean dirty cat boxes. I didn't share that joy, unless it was to perfect a technique in martial arts, so we were really a good team in that way. I did my share, but I wasn't a slave either.

All the same, this flurry of activity told me he was tired of being at home.

"So, you're really bored huh?" I queried, not letting on that I was impressed, bordering on slightly turned on, at how much he'd done around the house. He laughed, and that was the only answer he gave. I knew he was lovingly bored. He couldn't sit still for long, but he did love our family and home.

"Questions." This was our verbal shorthand. I was a woman of few words.

"Answers."

"How'd you know I was here? I mean, since I didn't use the door and all."

"It's my Spidey sense. I've been working on it," he said. So adorable.

"Do you know what Feng Shui means?"

"Um...Chinese something or other, meaning good placement of objects within a room or house?"

"Actually, partially yes. Very good." He was blowing my mind again by knowing anything about it whatsoever. "Literally, wind and water. Placement of objects designed to align the home with nature, and help the lives within to flow better in several areas."

"Yeah, this guy I worked with on the travel job talked to me about it one night, by the campfire. Really into it. He got some flack from the other guys for being into such things, but I just thought he was just spiritual and openminded. The mentality of a lot of these guys is to give others a bad time, instead of working together as a team. Another reason I want to come home and be with my team."

I told him about Jin's advice. He looked at me, smiled and shook his head. "Oddly, I so get that."

I breathed an inner sigh of relief. "I hoped you would. He offered to create a Zen garden in our backyard, and help find and place objects inside. He wanted to know if you'd a, be okay with it; b, want to help; or c, want to be working during the Feng Shui phase."

"A, yes, I'm quite okay with it; b, I'd like to help; c, I might not be able to help with the whole thing, because I'll have to go back to work; but d, I really want to, and I'm not just saying that."

"A, thank you; b, I'm so glad you're cool with this; c, I think it will enhance our lives in interesting, previously unforeseen ways; and d, I don't have a d."

"I love it when you talk like that," he said, putting down the silver and coming toward me.

"And if you don't like something, please by all means speak up. I don't wish to have anything here that you abhor." By that time, his hands were on my hips.

"Abhor is a good word."

"Abhor, abhor, abhor," I said, laughing. And he started kissing my collarbone.

"I'll show you some Feng Shui, Ninja Nanny," he said. And that was an offer I couldn't refuse.

We can always begin again.

Jack Kornfield

Chapter 6

Jin and I spent two weeks totally redoing the décor. We shopped at World Market, where Jin bought me all kinds of stuff, and I bought the rest that he said I needed. Hammer came with us for one of the trips, and picked out a laughing Buddha with children climbing on it. We ordered online from Gaiam.com and a few other sites. By the time we were finished, I had a whole bunch of stuff in the back of my hybrid Escape, and a bunch more on the way in the mail. I couldn't wait.

I'd gotten some orchids in a terra cotta pot, a lotus print, symbolizing perfection from impurity, as they grow in mud. I bought some yellow decorative sheets to put up on the walls in the kids' room, as the color symbolized motherhood. I got a mini Zen bonsai kit for the bedroom, which would be Yin energy for good rest which we both needed in this crazy world, some peacock feathers for protection, and a hammock to put outside between the only two trees in our yard. We got a jade dove, for longevity and health, and a turtle, sacred and symbolizing long life, wind chimes to put over the stove to double the money, and plenty of round mirrors, used to double income or deflect negative energy in a space. I needed something purple to put in the East corner, so I bought a lavender scented candle.

The feathers went in a big vase in the corner of the living room. We moved the desk from the bedroom into the living room, facing the water. A dragon and phoenix were placed into our bedroom, as these together were a traditional Chinese wedding gift, meaning harmonious partnership. The lotus print went in the dining room.

We worked tirelessly from morning until night. I helped Jin and Hammer get the sand for the Zen garden, and Jin showed us how to take care of it and we made patterns with the large wooden rake. We put a compost pile in the west corner. We'd gotten some mini-pagodas, which we placed near the Zen garden in that corner of the yard. The laughing Buddha also went outside in the yard, watching over everything. A Chinese unicorn went into the twins' room, as a sign of protection. The turtle went in the living room, and the dove in the kitchen, in the China cabinet.

We covered the televisions and the computer with sheets and put candles on top to hold them in place, as it's hard for the body to fully rest when technology items are fully visible. The television was on under the decorative sheet, so I went to turn it off and noticed the news was reporting another story of a child disappearing, this time in Colorado. These disappearances were disconcerting, and they went in a direct line by state. Only a few states away from us now.

Our last stop was the pet store. We were going to do a koi pond, but decided instead on a mini aquarium, as it helped the library Feng Shui and we had enough outside that the yard was perfectly full without being cluttered.

Jin showed me the Bagua diagram, and we walked around and looked at each area:

Prosperity
Fame
Relationships
Family/Growth
Health
Creativity/Children
Knowledge
Career
Helpful People/Travel

I had no idea there was so much to it.

Each area had an element, a number, a body part, a family member, a direction, and colors it corresponded to. I wasn't much of a natural Feng Shui person, apparently, because I had the wrong colors and elements everywhere, except for the new stuff we'd just bought.

Jin told me that the best times to work on Feng Shui were between a new moon and a full moon, and between eleven a.m. and one p.m. or eleven p.m. and one a.m. I was usually up taking care of the babies at that time, because they were still in odd stages of waking up, so it actually worked for me to be up in the night rearranging things. I worked on this constantly. If I'd been alone in trying to do the whole project, it would've been much harder to be motivated. But knowing Jin would inspect, I really worked at it, enlisting Hammer's help when he was home. I put some form of chime in every room, because using one or ringing a bell when you entered a room helped to clear the space.

After two more weeks of me doing my best to perfect the Feng Shui by reading about it, implementing what the books told me, and clearing all possible clutter, Jin said I had one more task to complete before officially starting Ninja training.

If a man is called to be a street sweeper,
he should sweep streets even as
Michelangelo painted,
or Beethoven composed music,
or Shakespeare wrote poetry.
He should sweep streets so well that all
the hosts of heaven and earth
will pause to say,
here lived a great street sweeper
who did his job well.

Martin Luther King Jr.

Chapter 7

"Cool, let's do it! Wait, what is it?"

"Okay. This one involves your stress level."

"Which is…"

"High at times, with occasional sun breaks." I bowed my head in admission, laughing.

"I'd like to help you reverse that, Phoenix," Jin said, looking earnest.

"How?"

"Come with me." It always secretly thrilled me when he said that. Where would we get to go this time?

"What's the busiest place you can think of?"

"New York City."

"Perfect."

Suddenly, there we were. I hadn't realized I could go this far. "Yes, you can," Jin said, penetrating my thoughts in his usual unnerving way. "Sorry," he said. I just laughed, looking around. We were a few blocks from the Trump Tower, which was enshrouded in fog.

"Wow!" The sights, sounds and smells were overwhelming. I heard sirens, talking, singing, yelling, selling, buying going on all around. Everyone was doing something different than everyone else—just like in Seattle, but the much more populated and fast-forwarded version. Tons of taxis and other vehicles raced by.

"Where's the Om, here?" For a moment I thought he was joking, because everything around us was bustling. Everything. But then I noted the serious expression on his face. "Take a moment to find it."

I knew what he meant. He meant to find the peace within the chaos. The stillness. The Om. I'd had this symbol tattooed on my left arm because I believed in it so deeply. We all needed to find our Om, our happy place.

I studied the scene. Hordes of people walked quickly by. Across the street, a limo waited for someone. Someone brushed past and bumped me, not apologizing. I felt thankful that during these teleporting sessions, we apparently didn't have to bring any money with us, and wonder if we could be seen and heard, since we could obviously be touched. It was total turmoil. But not total, because then I spotted the aforementioned Om.

"Viva la Vida" by Coldplay started playing, and I couldn't tell whether it was from inside my head or from someone's stereo, but it got louder.

"The man, there at the corner cafe, the one who's sweeping." The sign above the man's head said *Mr. Java. NYC's Best-Kept Secret.* His café was tiny compared to the surrounding businesses. We watched him for a moment. He was a bit removed from us, but I zoomed in, using my newfound Ninja skills. He hummed a tune, not seeming to mind at all that the world was passing his place by. He just kept on sweeping with a little smile on his face. He was old and had laugh lines, not stress lines, on his face. As if sensing our energy, he looked up and saw us, his smile suddenly widening. "He's a peaceful soul. I see the Om, and I see it in him," I continued. Some of his features made him look Spanish, but from different angles, Asian. I was sorry I wouldn't get to meet him.

"Excellent, Phoenix. Care for a coffee?" I looked at Jin, surprised. I didn't think we could actually talk to people. "We're good. I know him." Jin took my hand and we walked across the street. I guess since we'd been spotted, we couldn't exactly teleport on over without attracting attention.

We went in and Jin ordered us a couple of iced Americanos. He requested mine with sugar free vanilla, though I'd never told him I'd been drinking those, trying to avoid the extra calories after the twins were born. He just knew. "This is Mr. Java. He has owned this café for years and years," Jin introduced as I shook Mr. Java's hand. I felt the firm grip of a warrior in that handshake. Mr. Java smiled but remained silent.

Or rather, his lips didn't move. But he said, "Welcome, Phoenix. I've heard so much about you." "You can call me Hunter."

We sat down, drank our coffee and chatted about everything and nothing, all at once. And all without actually speaking!

Jin and Hunter led me through the double doors to what looked like the kitchen. Was I to learn some type of ethnic cooking?

My illusions of getting to cook were shattered as went through several more doors, and some winding hallways. Hunter stopped, faced Jin, handed him the key, and they bowed to each other. He brushed past me, and I noticed he seemed to glow. My eyes followed the light, and he disappeared leaving a cloud of golden specks of dust behind him. I smiled, because nothing was ever as it seemed, and I could count on that. The old-shopkeeper façade was just for appearances; Hunter was actually a mystical sage, of sorts. Jin unlocked the door, saying nothing.

He opened the door into a perfectly round room, made of glass. It was like stepping into a Christmas ornament, hanging in a rose-colored mist. He took my hand, and we floated up into the middle of it. My eyes filled with tears of wonder. I didn't know how this was possible.

"Phoenix, this is where our real journey begins. Look." The mist dissipated.

"Oh my God." I looked out the top of the sphere, and saw the world. It was like standing on the Space Needle where you could see all of Seattle, only this was the entire world!

"Your very own Google Earth," Jin said.

"Wuh…whoa."

"You can zoom in to anywhere."

I looked around, still floating, holding my trainer's hand. No one had ever given me the world before. I didn't quite know what to do with it. "Pick a place," he said. I thought of where I might never have the chance to go.

"Africa."

So we zoomed in to Africa, real time. We stood on the Serengeti Plains, watching the wildlife. It was just like *Wild Kingdom*—gazelles, lions, giraffes, elephants, a herd of hippos eating along the riverbank, the whole shebang. "They can see us just like humans can, right?" I asked.

"Yes. But not to worry, we can zoom out quickly too," Jin assured me, smiling.

"Okay, I think we should," I said, as the lions in the distance picked up our scent. I grabbed Jin's arm. He chuckled, closed his eyes and zoomed us out with his inner controls.

Back in the sphere, Jin explained that this was just a sample of what I could do, and that he would explain later what else was possible. On hearing this, I assumed he would issue me instructions at another time. I was thankful. I needed time to process that in a couple short hours I'd been to New York *and* Africa. I'd dreamed a jetsetter lifestyle, but had never gotten to experience one until now, and never thought it would be anything like *this*.

"Oh, we're just getting started, believe me," Jin said. This time his voice came from inside my head, where he was reading my thoughts. I knew I'd be getting used to this any time now.

"Why waste your breath, right?" I quipped.

"Precisely," he answered. "Plus, just in case people were ever eavesdropping, as they tend to do..." His voice trailed off, as we floated over to see Europe from afar.

"England?" I asked.

"Your wish is my command." And off we went, flying. Or floating, as it were. "Your task, same as before, is to find the Om. The place of peace within the chaos."

We landed in a park that Jin said was outside London. There were tons of kids playing, adults milling about, smoking and talking and laughing. Even though they were essentially still, they were busy in their own way.

"This may require some walking around to spot it," he said. So I started walking. The park was about two miles square. I watched some kids playing hopscotch. From their accents I could tell they were American. None of them had the Om I sought. Other kids played on some gym equipment—nope, not them either. I walked around and around, until I saw a man meditating. For a minute, I thought he had the Om, but then with my ninja-fied vision, I saw that he was deeply troubled. He was seeking peace, hadn't found it yet. Then I saw the men playing chess. They weren't just playing chess, but giant chess on a board that spread out between them of twenty feet. One of them was deep into the game and focused on winning. The other, though, he had a small smile much like Hunter's. He didn't care about winning; for him, it was all in the journey, not the destination.

"Jin!" I called in my mind. He came out from behind some trees, where he'd been trying not to distract my process. "I think I found it!"

"Good, Natalie, you sure did! You found not only the Om, but the false Om that was designed to throw you off."

"Designed? I thought these were real people, authentic situations. We're not in the Matrix, are we?"

"No, but there is a false sense of security in some people. It's only skin deep. I scanned the place quickly while you were walking around, and saw how some could view the meditating man as being at peace. Things are rarely as they seem on the surface, as you know, Phoenix. A job well done."

"Thank you." I wondered where we'd be going next.

Trust yourself.
You know more than
you think you do.

Dr. Spock

Chapter 8

In the sphere, fog ascended like a curtain around us. "Does this mean I'm going home now?" I asked, somewhat sadly. I wondered how the twins were doing, but knew Jade was watching them and doing a stellar job. She loved them like her own just as Jin did.

"Actually, no." Sifu smiled mysteriously. "We'll do something different now. Mix it up a little." God, how I loved him. I would never get bored with him around, ever.

He took my hands in his. "You felt the Om. Now can you feel the chaos?"

"What do you mean?"

"Can you feel someone needing you in the world right now?"

All at once I heard a million voices. It was so loud that I covered my ears for a second, and then realized they were coming from within. It was like the whole of New York City had been imported into my head and was crowding it, trying to escape.

"This time, find the opposite of Om, Phoenix."

I focused like I had done earlier, trying to pinpoint the chaos. Suddenly I heard it, and felt it.

"Boston. People in trouble. I can help. Can I go?"

"Yes, and I'll go with you."

We were in downtown Boston in front of a large apartment building on fire. Jin stood back. I surveyed the scene for a quick moment. The firefighters were there and people were trapped. I closed my eyes, scanning for where they were in the building, and after locating them, in I went.

They were in the basement laundry room, which was like a cave and nearly impossible to get to for the firefighters. But not for me. I beamed myself into the room. I found two young parents and their baby, huddled together as close to the ground as possible. Fortunately, the room was fireproof, being underground, but it was filling with smoke. They'd covered their baby's mouth and nose lightly with a handkerchief. The baby was awake but wide-eyed, fidgety, and scared. I told them I was there to get them out. I saw fear in their eyes but they were desperate so they had to trust me. Silently, they handed me their baby and I told them I'd be right back. I didn't exactly know where to put the baby, to remain unnoticed, but time was of the essence. So I beamed out of the building, gave the baby to Jin hoping he'd have a clue, and went back in to get the parents. I stood them up, put my arms around their shoulders, closed my eyes and we were outside the building, looking up at it burning. Jin met me with the baby, and I ushered the couple towards an ambulance. The wife hugged me hurriedly, and they staggered towards the flashing lights.

Then Jin hugged me, which, by the way, was great because I was shivering and sweating, all at once. I had done my job efficiently, and now it was time for me to fall apart. He gathered me into his arms, which felt like wings around me, and we reconvened at the sphere. "You can call this home base," he said.

Colin materialized before my eyes. "Phoenix," he said, smiling.

I smiled in response. I was without words at this time. He put his arm around me, brought me to the opposite side of the sphere, and we melted into the floor. It was like we were on an invisible elevator and went down a level.

He rubbed my shoulders and told me the sphere was not only home base but healing base. He gave me a purple health drink. "Blueberries," he said, and told me to sip it while in the hot springs. Hot springs?? Yep, this sphere deal was fully loaded.

While I soaked, Jin's voice came into my head. He said I needed to consider what'd happened as more than a good deed I did once. See how I felt about it being my destiny in life to do this.

Whoa. I didn't know how to process this. I mean, my *destiny*. That was a lot to take in while the sweat was pouring out of my soul. His voice then said I didn't have to process it right here and now, but take some time and think about the implications of what it would mean for my life.

I started thinking about it instantly, even though I was sweating buckets. Why did I have to learn to throw Ninja stars, if this was my destiny? Jin's voice answered me right away. "Throwing Ninja stars teaches you precision in your aim. And you haven't learned everything yet." A small laugh followed. Apparently I had more to learn. I was so cool with that fact. I wanted to learn everything *now*! But from past experience with Jin and Jade, and even from my trip with Sam, I knew everything came in its own time. The universe's time.

"That was crazy intense," I said, snapping back into the present moment. "Can we do that again, Sifu? Can we, can we, pleeeeease?"

Jin laughed. "Maybe someday soon. For now, we have other work to do. I'll see you in a couple days." Ah! Always an air of mystery surrounded my mentor. I wouldn't have it any other way. But I still wanted to know more about him, and vowed to find the courage to ask.

Water,
everywhere over the earth,
flows to join together.
A single natural law controls it.

Each human is a
member of a community and should
work within it.

I Ching

Chapter 9

I got home, and by that I mean I was beamed home in a burst of teleportation awesomeness. I released Jade from babysitting duty, read a note from Hammer that he'd be home late afternoon, put the twins on a blanket on the floor with a few toys and let them play while I watched them. About half an hour later, I fed them and put them in their crib and kissed them goodnight after another really exhausting day, and fell fast asleep on the floor beside their crib.

When I opened my eyes, Jin and I stood behind a waterfall. As in, inside of one, facing out. Behind us, cave wall. In front of us, water wall. "Phoenix, your first challenge as a ninja is to walk through it without getting wet." He paused, sensing my doubt. "Don't put your energy into doubting. Put it into *doing*."

Best. Advice. Ever. So I surveyed the scene in front of me. Usually, I did this straight away as Jin had trained me. The moment I opened my eyes to a new place, I knew where every person and object in it was instantly, and if something was off, kind of like in the movie *XXX*, when Vin Diesel pointed out what was wrong. I was like my old friend Vin doing a Sherlock scan in that movie. My spidey sense was off the hook! This was a basic martial arts skill, and made for efficient fighting. This time though, I didn't want to lose my footing. The waterfall flowed in such a way that the ground level didn't change directly on the other side of it, so I'd be able to just step through.

"Keep it simple, sweetheart," I thought to myself.

"Exactly," Jin said. "Start with your hand."

I held my right hand up and out, visualizing it coming out dry on the other side. I stuck it through, and it was sopping wet. "Damn," I swore under my breath, wiping off my hand on my shirt.

"Visualize no waterfall, just air. You must make peace with the elements before doing anything else."

I tried again, sticking my hand out. I pushed through, and felt water again.

"Summon the air, Phoenix." So I took a deep breath, filling my lungs with misty air, asking it respectfully to cooperate and surround the water, and slowly put my hand through. It worked! I pulled my hand back through, and jumped up and down, hugging Jin, who laughed at my excitement. I never knew if he was laughing at, with, or near me. But this time it didn't matter. I'd done it!

"Now, try this. It will be harder, as it's not part of you, but will not be impossible. Nothing is." He handed me a sword. I didn't know where it came from, as I hadn't seen him holding it. I grasped it and felt its weight. Doing the same visualizing of air around the sword, and summoning of the air and water to cooperate with each other and with me while not disrupting anything around us, I stuck the tip through.

It didn't get wet! I kept going, piercing the water with the sword, and pushed it all the way through without getting it or my hand wet.

"Excellent, Phoenix. Now, walk through."

I took the deepest breath I'd ever taken to date, handed him the sword, and stepped through the waterfall. I blinked and examined myself. My arm was still damp from the first effort, but I did not have a drop of water on me. I whirled and looked at Jin, who smiled. "Congratulations." I hugged him.

"You did very well today." He stepped through, completely dry after, as if this were the easiest thing in the world to do, and splashed me playfully. "We'll work with each element in its various forms for five days. Tomorrow, ice." I wondered if the Wonder Twins would show up to help us.

"Probably not them, Phoenix, but you may have help from sources other than myself." He smiled, eyes flashing his eternal enigmatic brand of humor.

As soon as I saw you,
I knew an adventure
was going to happen.

Winnie the Pooh

Chapter 10

I was nervous to work with air. It was the element I was least comfortable with. Fire, I had been in close contact with. Fire, Jin told me I didn't have to work with at all because I was impermeable to it already. Water was my element of choice, so it didn't faze me. Earth might be a challenge. But air? I didn't want to try to fly, and why was I required to, when I already knew how to teleport? Leave the flying to Superman, I say. At the waterfall I had summoned the air while working water, but never air by itself, and I just wasn't comfortable with it. I needed to practice before Jin and I met, which would feel like a test of my skills. That was fine; it had its place. But I needed to consult with someone who could fly.

I didn't know who to ask or who'd show up. Orville and Wilbur Wright would not be quite appropriate. I needed someone who could teach me about the kinds of flying you do with your body and some ropes and a parachute.

Jin's words echoed in my mind. "You must make peace with the elements before doing anything else." Make peace, huh? Alrighty, then. I made sure the twins and kitties were fine and sleeping, and stepped inside the bathroom. Oddly, that's where the best summoning took place.

With the sudden urge to shower overtaking me, I hopped in. Surrounded by water, I felt most at home and at peace. No problem making peace with water. I let it just roll down my back and let the steam surround me without opening the bathroom window as I usually did. I began to think about how to make peace with, or become one with, air. I had never enjoyed flying in planes. It was thrilling, but the minute the turbulence started, I was toast.

Enjoying the immense heat, I let go of the anxiety, closed my eyes, and opened them again and the steam had turned into a syrupy fog. I found myself on top of a mountain. The fog cleared enough for me to look down and see that I was in a white, glittery bodysuit. *I've morphed into a female snow beast*, I thought.

"Not hardly," a voice replied out of the air. It wasn't Jin's. In fact, I thought I detected a familiar British accent. "Spot on, love."

I had no idea where I was, and thought some prep for this might've been nice. But I had learned that was not the way the cards were dealt in the superhero world. I was on a mountain in a bodysuit being spoken to by a voice inside my head who was reading my mind, and that's just how it was for me. Good heavens, at least I wasn't naked.

I noticed that I wasn't freezing or even slightly cold, and the voice said my bodysuit was impermeable to weather and weapons. I couldn't help wondering if I would get to keep it after this episode was over.

I heard throaty laughter coming from whoever this was, spying on me from wherever he was. And then through his laughter, which somehow sounded like Christmas bells in a very good way, he apologized, realizing he was still invisible, and appeared.

As I live and breathe, I thought, as my eyes glazed over from shock. Sitting there, big as life, in a clearing on the mountain, on an ocean blue-colored round yoga mat, was Mr. Gordon Sumner, aka Sting.

"Join me," he beckoned, "for a bit of yoga?"

Now how could I resist an offer like that?

So he unrolled a yoga mat for me and I sat. It was a round yoga mat like his, only mine was a deep violet. I had never seen circular mats before. "We're just going to work on breathing. We're not going to fly. I'm here to teach you some preliminary steps," he explained, as if all of this was completely natural. I couldn't wipe the smile off my face for a million bucks.

We sat, and he taught me how to breathe deep, deep within my belly, bringing it into my chest so it was full of air. We went through a series of poses and he instructed me on how to deepen them, what to focus on as I was breathing into the pose. I was nervous at first, doing yoga in front of a mega-super rock star/yogi. But then, I got over it. I couldn't really help it, because we were speeding up the yoga now and sweating from the exertion.

I was good with doing hot yoga on a freezing mountaintop with Sting. Sometimes though, I just wished I could tell my friends. I heard him chortle under his breath. "You can tell Hammer, and Sam too if you like," he said. I was too stunned at having my mind read by Sting to answer. Not to mention too out of breath.

Finally, he slowed the pace to a much more reasonable one, and then at last we lay there side by side in stillness.

"Why the round yoga mats and not rectangular?"

"Round is better Feng Shui. Curves have no angles. Angles create poison arrows that point at others."

"Yes," I said. "The world, in all its roundness, is very angular, isn't it?"

"Indeed it is," he said. "Thank you, Natalie. I've enjoyed our little lesson."

"Me too. Thank you." We silently stood and bowed to each other the way yogis do. It was a different sort of bow from the way my sifu and I bowed, much more informal and quick, but still showing respect.

Sting faced me and looked me directly in the eyes. "Visualize all of the things that stress you out, all of the problems and conundrums you can't figure out. Bring them to the forefront of your mind. Acknowledge them, and let them go. See them fading from your vision as they drop away. Watch them being swallowed by the earth. See the earth stitching itself up where they went through, and know that they can never come back. Whatever presents itself to you from now on is a challenge and not a problem.

"You will know inherently how to deal with each challenge as it comes, and you will deal with them one at a time, without being overwhelmed as you have been. If you per chance don't know how to deal with them, you shall have help, so remember not to panic."

"I shall have help," I repeated to myself.

The way he said this made me feel very calm and very light. Before I knew it, I was back on my yoga mat, next to Sting on his yoga mat, and I heard his voice telling me to relax and go with the flow. And I did. And it was good. As a moist, soft mist enveloped me, I faded into it willingly.

The mist subsided and I drifted over an ocean that I recognized at once. It was the same ocean whose waves massaged the shores where the pagoda was. I found myself waving hello to Jade, who smiled up at me, but I didn't land there, just passed it on by. I floated on just like the Modest Mouse song says we all do. But wait, I wasn't floating; I was flying! I was flying. It felt a lot like swimming. I was weightless, but could hear and feel the wind all around me.

"See Phoenix, not everything is as difficult as you think," Sting's voice echoed in my ears.

I nodded in agreement and did some flips and turns in the sky, because now, somehow, I could. "I take back the Superman comment," I said, my voice sounding very echo-chambery. He laughed with delight at my discovery. Right then, I flew inside a cloud, which was moist but oddly warm. I felt the vapor start to surround me like I was being cocooned, and too tired to fight it, relaxed into the sensation.

When I awoke, I was not back in the shower but instead next to my own fireplace, curled up in a blanket. I heard crackling and smelled smoke, and saw that there was in fact a fire burning in the fireplace. *What a nice way to wake up. I wonder what's in store for me that I have such nice moments...*

"Don't worry yourself, love," Sting's voice soothed, from afar. "You get yanked from your life, showering or not. This is just our way of paying it back. Enjoyyy it," he said, his voice fading, which made me sad. I wouldn't get to make him tea or show him around my newly Zenned-out house or ask what his superpowers were.

"Thanks, Mr. Sumner," I said to the retreating image of Sting on the mountaintop in my mind.

"Call me Gordon," he replied. I could almost hear the smile in his voice and see his eyes sparkling with humor.

I laughed slightly, too exhausted to find a response, relieved Hammer wasn't home to hear what would've sounded like me talking to myself. Yanked from showers, indeed. Which reminded me, what was I wearing? I peeked under the blanket. No snow beast attire, no nothing. I giggled to myself, and, knowing Jade was watching the kids, noting my own extreme mental and physical exhaustion, fell directly to sleep.

I awoke to the sound of Hammer coming in and felt him kiss my forehead, then heard the shower go on. I remembered, somewhere in the recesses of my sleeping mind, that he had just worked one of his long shifts and would likely be exhausted. *I should really get up and defrost dinner,* I remember thinking, before falling immediately back to sleep. I had made a creative casserole, and was looking forward to having us try it with some wine I'd bought. Hammer loved my cooking, which was a bonus.

"Mmmmm….me*ow*! We love your cooking too, Nnnnnatalie," Claw said. "Please share at your convenience."

Laughing, I answered that I'd see what I could do. He nuzzled me and crawled onto my stomach. "Nice and ssssquishy, just like I like it," he remarked, while Kiki came and rested at my feet. She looked up at me, winked her blue eye, rested her head on a paw and started purring. I woke myself up giggling at my precious feline furbabies. I would always have a special love for them, as they had been my children before I had real children. It was dark outside, and I wondered what time it was. Checking my cellphone, I found that it was already the middle of the night so I started to get up to check on the kids and join Hammer in bed when a voice from the couch said "Not so fast, kunoichi. We have one more thing to learn tonight."

It wasn't Jin. It wasn't Vin. It wasn't Yoda. It wasn't Sting. It most definitely wasn't Hammer. He had used the term for female ninja, so it was someone who knew of such things. But process of elimination was leading me nowhere. I was nervous, hoping I wasn't confronting an enemy without warning, while naked. This wasn't good…

Once you have tasted flight,
you will forever walk the earth
with your eyes turned skyward,
for there you have been,
and there you will always
long to return.

Leonardo Da Vinci

Chapter 11

"Sorry to barge in on you like this."

It was Hunter. Mr. Java himself. A wave of relief
washed over me that it wasn't the enemy tonight. I got
up to greet him. "Yes, and welcome. Would you mind if
I excuse myself for a moment first to…" my voice
trailed off. I needed to find something suitable to wear
for…wait, what were we going to be doing, training, at
this hour? I wondered to myself. I'd been wondering
that quite a lot lately.

"No training," he said. "But yes, let's get you
dressed."

And suddenly, I was dressed. I sported a form-fitting black leather bodysuit and a matching backpack. I felt very insulated and protected as well as accessorized. I really wished I could keep some of these outfits.

"You have access to all the attire you've worn since becoming a ninja," he said.

"I…do?"

"Why yes. I thought you knew. It's in the pagoda, in your closet there."

"I have a closet in the pagoda??" I was stunned. I wondered if I pushed on a panel in the back of my closet, like in the Chronicles of Narnia, would I reach this magnificent and wondrous wardrobe?

"All you need to do is make your way to the pagoda, and you have a full range of attire, both for fighting and ceremonies. So basically, all of your body suits and body armor and weaponry items are there. And let us not forget the footwear. It's more than a wardrobe. It's an arsenal."

"Oh my," I said. Of all of the surprises I'd encountered thus far in my ninja life, this was the one that made me a super-excited superhero. Shoes. Boots. Knives, swords. I didn't have a Batcave, but I had a wardrobe arsenal. Even better!

"Your wardrobe is attached to a suite of rooms. You have this at your disposal," he said.

My jaw just about dropped to the floor.

"Your house here is your launch pad. But you have a husband and children and cats. Lots of, for lack of a better word, distractions. Your suite of rooms is your think pad. You can use it to train, to sleep, or to just get away. Time passes very slowly in that realm, so if you think you're gone for five hours, you may be actually gone five minutes here. It's how superheroes get things done," he said, dimples flashing.

I gave myself a moment to center and take it in. I didn't have to worry so much about inconveniencing Jin and Jade by calling upon them as babysitters. "Are you my new sifu?" I asked, puzzled as to why this was coming from him instead of Jin.

"No, I am simply here to teach you what Jin and Jade do not have time to. Think of me as a visiting professor," he said. I liked his humor. I could tell he was a hardened warrior with a softer side that he presented to most of the world. The softer side was the man I'd seen, sweeping outside the café. The warrior he kept well hidden and pulled out for emergencies only.

"Very perceptive, kunoichi," he said, a small smile playing upon his lips. I noticed how much his eyes resembled those of Tommy Lee Jones.

"Sorry, I didn't mean to pry," I apologized, blushing a bit at having him decipher that I was reading him.

"Never apologize; this is a worthy skill and deserves developing."

I was about to ask Hunter if I could go see this wardrobe of maximum coolness of which he spoke, but remembered he said I had something to learn tonight.

"Come, we'll learn on the way," he said, gesturing me out the sliding glass door. He was surprisingly quick. He wore a Dracula-like cape. It rippled behind him with the breeze as he walked, furthering the air of mystery about this man.

We walked to an open field in a park nearby. No one was there. I was really glad I trusted Jin and his friends, because it was a windy, slightly scary night and here I was standing outside with someone I'd only met once who was dressed like Dracula and could read my mind.

"Okay, Natalie. We're going to the pagoda to pick up some things you'll need in the near future."

"Are we going to teleport?"

"No, we're going to fly," he replied matter-of-factly. He took my hands, and without warning, we flew through the night. It was thrilling. We flew and flew under the cloudless sky, and the outfit I had on kept me insulated. He held one of my hands and then suddenly slowed his speed.

"If you ever fatigue while flying, which happens sometimes even to superheroes, you can do the equivalent of treading water in the air. You don't have to flail about, just lightly move around, sort of like dancing." He demonstrated how to do this, and I mirrored his movements. "That's right," he encouraged. "This will replenish your energy quickly. Now, let's go," he directed, and again we soared.

One of the greatest discoveries
a man makes,
one of his greatest surprises,
is to find he can do
what he was afraid he
couldn't do.

Henry Ford

Chapter 12

I could see the pagoda below. "Okay, now I'm going to teach you how to land. Before, you practiced and didn't have to land by yourself, but it can be a bit tricky. The gravity of earth pulls you to it, so you have to slow yourself down. It's a mental process. So visualize whatever helps you do this…I usually attach myself to some cords which are attached to a cloud, in here anyway," he said, pointing to his temple.

I tried the visualization trick, because we were coming in at a pretty good clip towards land. It worked! I was actually slowing down.

"The actual landing process is a lot like skydiving, if you've ever done that," he said.

"Can't say as I have," I said, a tremor in my voice.

Chuckling, he advised me to not lock my legs, and do a tuck-and-roll type thing if I went too fast in the future. It seemed to be going well this time, though. He grabbed my hand and we landed together in the sand on the beach. I wobbled, but didn't fall. Sand was nice to land on, but I could imagine cement and other such surfaces would pretty much suck.

We followed the lights shining through the forest to the pagoda. Jade was there to welcome us. "Hunter," she said, embracing him as though they hadn't seen each other for a long time.

Jade turned to me, explaining that they had worked together on some special projects back in the day. I wondered if I'd ever get to hear about them.

"All in due time, Phoenix," Hunter said, but he wasn't speaking. He had answered my nonverbal query nonverbally. I guessed that was allowed. "Speaking of work, we have some to do here tonight." We walked through the pagoda in silence, going up the elevator to the fourth floor and down hallways I didn't recognize. This pagoda was enormous inside.

Jade led the way into my suite, which had its own foyer, and through into the bedroom. The bed was king-sized, with a gorgeous canopy, unlike anything I'd ever seen. This wasn't mosquito netting but a thick blend of cotton. One half was black and one was white, not split down the middle but diagonally. It was as close to a yin/yang design that a rectangular canopy could get. There were wood floors, and huge double-paned windows. The one on the east side looked out over the ocean. Off to the west there was a room with a writing desk and a bay window. The bathroom had a two-person jet tub and all modern appliances—nothing like the Japan I remembered. But a) my parents weren't rich; and b) this wasn't really Japan. It was a place in another realm, not on any map.

We adjourned to what looked like normal closet doors. Hunter opened them with a grandiose gesture, and the closet inside was empty, but mirrored. We faced our reflections, and I thought this was a good trick, as an intruder might scare himself for a moment. I looked at Hunter's reflection, awaiting an explanation or some instructions.

He looked at me intently, and told me my pass code. It was "ninjacats." I smiled. He said it had to come from me, but I didn't see any keypad or other place to enter a pass code. He explained that I just had to say it. It wouldn't open to anyone's voice but mine.

"Oh," I said. I was glad this pass code didn't require special characters or numbers. *Ninjacats capital N star underscore umlaut five thousand* or something similar would have really sucked to try to recall, but by itself was cake.

"Ninjacats."

The back of the closet opened up, doors sliding with that cool noise like you hear in the movies when an ancient vault is unsealed. In front of us was a set of stone steps going up, and the walls on either side were brick. It really did smell ancient in here.

"That's because no one has been in here for centuries," Jade said.

"But there are clothes and things somewhere in here, right? How did they get in here?" I wondered.

Every time an outfit appears on you, when you no longer need it for the time being, it appears here. Also, we sort of "order" things for you, knowing what is coming. So we just supply your wardrobe and arsenal for you.

"What is coming?" I asked, with utmost curiosity.

"It's not time yet for you to know," Hunter answered. "Jin will be having that conversation with you when it is."

I took a deep breath and exhaled slowly. Patience wasn't one of my virtues. "Understood."

"Now," Hunter said, with maximum drama, "to your wardrobe, Ms. Newport."

He opened the door to the top of the stairs, and before me was the most impressive wardrobe/arsenal I had ever seen. Never mind that it was also the *only* wardrobe/arsenal I had ever seen!

In front of me was every kind of leather suit, bodysuit, and item of workout attire I could imagine. Sam and I had joked about me having a closet full of leather, but this was a different kind—true fighting gear. The other half of the moon was composed of evening attire as well as geisha outfits galore, all of which put last year's Halloween costume to shame. The evening wear went from sophisticated to plain, but with a plunging neckline. And there was a Catholic schoolgirl outfit— the white buttoned shirt, the pleated skirt, thigh highs, the whole bit. I looked at Hunter and Jade. "Really?"

"We threw that in for Hammer. Thought he might like it," Hunter said, eyes full of mischief. Jade giggled. I joined her.

And then there were the shoes. I had boots of about ten different styles and lengths, from combat to come hither. There were athletic shoes of all different colors and styles. I picked some up and looked at the size, which was, of course, mine. There were also plenty of dress shoes, all matching the evening outfits. I noticed four-inch stilettos under the schoolgirl outfit. "And schoolgirls wear stilettos, these days?"

"Well, some do, and this one will," Hunter answered.

"Fair enough," I said, amused and incredulous about all of this, still feeling I was in a dream and would awake at any second. Hunter instructed me to say my pass code again, twice. "Ninjacats ninjacats," I said, in a sort of hushed whisper of excited anticipation. I heard a sound like air being compressed, which sounded sort of like "schewwww," and instantly, doors slid across all of the compartments and closed in front of me, and the compartments slid to the side.

The next layer of closet space contained floor-to-ceiling weaponry—an entire collection of different swords or katanas—medium-length blades, of different styles and designs, as well as an entire wall of shuriken. I daresay there were about eighty styles of stars, maybe more. Some were two-dimensional, some were three. There were projectiles of all kinds, blowpipes to shoot them from, bows and arrows, darts, climbing and scaling tools, gunpowder weapons and knuckle-dusters, or hand claws, as well as finger claws. There were rope ladders and blades of many different types, and spikes for climbing and foodstuffs, vacuum-packed and sealed for…days of eating on the fly, it seemed.

Hunter had been watching me study the arsenal before us. I looked at him intently, wondering if he was sure he didn't want to tell me what I was apparently destined to be up against. "It's not that I don't want to, Phoenix," he said. "It's that I am not allowed to. It has to be Jin, for some reason I can't explain."

"Okay. I am extra curious now after seeing all of this. It's everything one would need to…" my voice trailed off into distraction. I would have to talk to Jin at earliest convenience.

"Yes, it is, but you won't need all of it for this mission," he finished.

"Are you clear on how to get here, and how to get in here?" Hunter asked.

"Yes."

"Okay. My work here is done, for now…" he said. Always the mystery of what was to come.

"Is it okay if I sleep here, now?" I asked.

"Yes," Jade answered. I looked around and suddenly noticed that Hunter was gone. "You can sleep as long as you want, you will only be gone for minutes, on your time." We made our way back down the stairs and into my bedroom. "You'll see a very normal dresser in the writing room there," she pointed. "No secret compartments or pass codes, just normal clothes for lounging, all in your size," she said with a comforting smile.

"Thank you, Jade," I said. We bowed to each other and she left the room. I loved bowing, but I still thought hugs were better, no matter the culture.

I sat on my bed in silence for a moment, taking it all in. In the dresser, I found a beautiful silky silver negligee that fit perfectly, so after changing into it, I gazed out at the hypnotic ocean for a good little while, and fell fast asleep.

Calm the winds
of your thoughts,
and there will be no waves
on the ocean of your
mind.

Anonymous

Chapter 13

I awoke from a dream-filled sleep, having had one continuous dream of flying over the ocean. I just studied the water and land formations of islands, and somehow knew the topography of this place, wherever or whenever it was, like the back of my hand after waking. I remember not knowing where to land, and glancing behind me to see attached a pair of clear crystalline wings, and then waking up. There was a ton of sleep sand in my eyes, so for a moment I couldn't open them, and I wondered, during that moment, where I was. Had I teleported in my sleep, back home from the pagoda? Was this possible?

I heard the pitter patter of little kitty feet, and some meowing and some sounds coming from the bathroom that sounded unquestionably like Hammer. So apparently, not only was it possible, but I had done it.

"Morning, angel," Hammer said, coming out of the bathroom.

"Morning babe," I said, stretching. "How are the twins?"

"They're fine. Magically, somehow still asleep. You appeared about two hours ago. I crashed early last night, but felt your presence when you came in."

"Or…came back," I said, smiling. "I was at the other place," I said. That's how he and I referred to it. He used to worry a lot when I was suddenly gone in the night, but had calmed down about it when I explained the other place. He still did worry though, as I worried about him when he was suddenly gone in the night even though I knew why.

"Ah, I see. Good session?"

"Oh, yes," I said. "I was finally provided with some clues as to what this whole Ninja Nanny thing is about."

"Well that's great! Are you allowed to share?"

"I am, but I'm not going to yet. Not until I get some answers from Jin."

"Cool. Let me know, when you find out," he said. "I've been trying to figure out my Ninja Nanny for quite some time now."

I grabbed the other pillow and tossed it at him.

"Just teasing, of course. I love you, Natalie," he said.

"I love you too, firefighter extraordinaire," I replied. He started to kiss me like he meant business, but we heard baby noises from next door so I got up to see what was needed, and that was the end of that.

"Plans for today?" Hammer asked, coming into the baby room.

"I thought I'd take the twins for a walk in the doublewide," I said.

"Sounds like fun. Want company?"

"Sure." I was thrilled to have my husband home and be able to actually hang out with my family. I so hoped Hammer wouldn't get an emergency call on one of his rare days off.

I showered and Hammer bundled up the babies. They looked adorable in their hats and scarves and their own individual fleece binkies. Hammer had a natural flair with kids that he was unaware of. I kissed him just before we went out the door. We probably looked like an advertisement for fleece winter wear, but none of us would get cold.

We walked the sidewalk to the park by the water, and down onto the dock. There were a few families and individual walkers out, but not many.

The twins seemed thrilled to be out. Hammer ran to get us a couple coffees, and I waited at a picnic table. I'd been learning so much lately that these more commonplace moments were something I really relished. I found in them little miracles, because they were so rare in my world—the chance to just be a mom and wife for a bit, and bask in the love of my family.

Hammer came back with my drink of choice, and Tim. "Look who I found!"

"Tim!" I said, embracing Hammer's longtime co-worker and friend, who had been in the background when Hammer proposed. "It feels like forever. How have you been?"

"Oh, pretty good. Just trying to stay warm these days," he said. He looked good. Happy.

"Oh, yeah? And is there anyone helping you do that?" I said, making him blush.

He stammered some sort of reply, which was half laugh, half gibberish, when Hammer came to his aid. "Tim is indeed seeing someone," he said.

"Well? Who is the lucky lady?" I said.

"Her name is Tarah," he said. His eyes got all shiny and as I read his face it was sort of glowing.

"You should bring her over some night," I said, Hammer nodding. "We'll cook up something delicious."

"Or at least edible. Let's not shoot for the moon here, Natalie," he said. I swatted him. "Just kidding, it'll be scrumptious."

Tim sounded really excited as he agreed and we parted ways.

Hammer and I talked about the meal possibilities on the way back to the car. We were getting pretty decent at preparing meals together. We got home and put the kids to bed for their nap, which they were ready for early because of the excitement of being outside. I knew Hammer wanted some alone time with me, as I did with him. But I needed to hit the gym, and he knew that so he didn't push it.

I teleported there, and worked out for about an hour. I was still unsure about what to do for a living, not having much time to spare, because I was determined to be my own nanny and not hire one, but could spend a little less time at the gym and attend some classes if need be. Going back to school wasn't a bad idea for a career that made us more money. Hammer made plenty at the local department to support us, but we weren't putting any away for our later years or for our kids' futures and it bothered me. I just wondered how to balance it all.

Plus, what to get Hammer for Christmas this year? His birthday in September had been challenging enough, and now it was nearly December. Jeeze. I found myself going faster and faster on the elliptical as my mind raced, trying to think of solutions.

I felt a hand on my back, turned around, and it was Jin. "You want to take a break for a few?" he said. "I'll buy you a smoothie from the café. Looks like you could use one."

Seeing something in his eyes that told me not to argue, I agreed. "Sure, let me towel off and I'll be right in."

Call it a clan,
call it a tribe,
call it a network,
call it a family.
Whatever you call it,
whoever you are,
you need one.

Jane Howard

Chapter 14

As I sat to join him, I noticed Jin had a more serious look on his face than I'd ever seen. If this was to be the talk about what I was doing next, I should be scared, I thought. That look was intense.

"It's not time for you to know yet, Natalie," he advised, reading my thoughts as usual and therefore knowing that I was getting rather tired of hearing this. "But the reason I look so serious is this. You *must* go easier on yourself. You are evolving at a perfectly acceptable pace, into your destiny and your life with Hammer. You can't know, or do, everything all at once."

"Yes, Sifu," I said, bowing my head, guilty as charged. I did want to advance, and didn't want to be held back.

"I know we've had this talk before," he said. "I tell you this not to scold you, but to remind you that stressing out in such a way depletes your chi, the energy you'll need for other things."

"I can appreciate that," I replied. "I just get anxious. About *everything*."

"I know, Little Phoenix," he said, using this term of endearment for the second time ever with me. "Just let it go." I took a deep breath and exhaled. "Just let it go," he repeated. The second time he said it, we were suddenly in the training studio downstairs. He took me in his arms, and I took a deep breath in, and out, and sobbed. I let it all out. I think all the tension had just built up inside me, like a giant iceberg, and now it was melting...all over Jin.

"I'm sorry," I said.

"Natalie, it's okay. It's all going to be okay," he said. Sometimes, we just need to hear that in life. "Breathe."

I worked on evening out my breathing. I was embarrassed at breaking down like this in front of him—the one who was supposed to have utmost confidence in me and think I was strong. "Do you have more to teach me today?"

"Not teach, just tell," he said.

"Okay." I was calming down, so I thought I could handle whatever this might be.

We sat facing each other. He took my hands. "You have a sister," he said.

"I...*what???*"

"You have a sister. Your parents couldn't afford to take care of two children when you all lived in Japan."

I thought about this. I couldn't remember ever having a sibling. I didn't have a lot of memories of Japan because we'd moved to the States when I was five, but I did remember living there in general, and sort of scrolled through my mental movie reel—granted, that of the mind of a child, but I couldn't bring up the memory of any other girls around.

"It would've been too early for you to remember. Your parents did something many would consider controversial, and gave her to some friends who couldn't conceive children but desperately wanted kids. They took care of her, or were planning to, until she was old enough to be on her own. She was...a bit of a rebel, and struck out on her own at age sixteen, determined to find her family."

Sixteen. This was the same age I was when my parents were killed in a boating accident.

"Your parents desperately wanted to raise the both of you together, but they just couldn't. Then when they heard she'd left home, you can imagine how much they wanted to get her back. To bring her here, where they felt she would have more opportunities in life, and where you could all live together. And then..." he trailed off, not wanting to bring it up.

"...The accident," I finished for him. "I see. So what happened to her? Where did she go?"

"I watched her grow into a strong young woman. She worked down by the docks for a year or so trying to earn enough for the trip home, always having had a love of water. She wanted to be as close to it as possible."

She had a love of water. Hmm, this was sounding more and more oddly familiar, in a very parallel universe kind of way.

"She showed her strength and proved her work ethic for long enough that the men aboard one of the ships wanted to hire her. She named her price, and they agreed. So she became a pirate. She has been sailing the seas for several years now, and knows all the things that pirates do. She meant to find you, but just sort of got stuck going through the motions and caught up in life."

"Is she...to be trusted?" I asked, hoping the answer was yes.

"She is. Your sister is tough, but trustworthy. She doesn't steal or pillage like some pirates, just sails the seas in search of treasure, knowing her lifestyle is the true treasure in the end, because she loves it so much. She will haggle over the slightest detail if she feels it is off, and she is very protective of those she loves."

"Does she have children? A husband?"

He closed his eyes for a moment, focusing. "I can't see those details, just that she is alive and still at sea."

"Her name?"

"Nozomi," Jin said. "It means 'hope.' Your parents wanted to give one of you a Japanese name since you and she were born there.

I could have sworn he was having me on until this point in the conversation. It was obvious he wasn't, now, so I sat and digested the information in silence. I had a pirate sister with a Japanese name. "Does she look like me?"

"She is your twin. Identical," he said, sensing my next question. I'm sure my eyes were as wide as quarters. Having a twin sister was a surprise I wasn't expecting. Finding out about her after this long was definitely a shock. "She looks almost exactly like you, but the hair color is different. Hers is lighter," he said. "Like your mother's." It stood to reason, since I took after my father, at least in looks. He had been dark, and she'd been more fair, from what I remembered. There were few pictures of our family in existence. I guess they weren't big on family photography.

"So, apparently twins run in the family then," I said, thinking of my own and that I should really get home to check on them.

"Indeed they do," Jin said with a sparkle in his eye. He knew more that he wasn't telling me, or for some reason couldn't tell me. "I know you have to get home, it's not like you're on Pagoda time right now," he said. "And by the way, I do think you're strong, Natalie. Immensely strong."

"Thank you, Sifu," I said. We stood bowed to each other, and I was instantly home, just inside my front door. Phew, no transition time.

"Hi, babe," Hammer said. "I was just getting ready to call you. I got called in early."

"Ah, okay. Do you need anything?"

"Nope, I'm good. Got my lunch packed," he said, which really meant his dinner. This was usually the way with us. One of us was always getting called to our job, or in my case, catapulted to my destiny. I wanted to tell him my news, but it would have to wait. He kissed me and left. I fed the kids and kitties and then called Sam. I had to tell someone, and she was the closest thing to a relative I had. Well, up to this point at least.

Sam was as floored as I had been, and asked questions before I could even get the answers out. She asked if I was going to meet her, and I said yes, but I wasn't sure when. I didn't know where to find her yet. It would seem that my spidey ninja sixth sense would kick in, to be able to find my twin. But I was getting nothing. No vibes.

I asked her how she was, and she said she was surrounded by firefighters, day in and day out so things could be worse. I laughed, knowing exactly what she meant and missing for a moment our adventures on the road. We agreed and that we definitely needed a visit but neither one of us was sure when we were going to be traveling here or there, and hung up.

Well, now I was sitting here wondering how to find my sister, and wondering if she knew about me, and if she also had superpowers, and all of the other questions I'd forgotten to ask. Damn.

The possession of knowledge
does not kill
the sense of wonder and mystery.
There is always more
mystery.

Anais Nin

Chapter 15

"Mmmmmmmmmmmreowwwww...Mnatalie Mnatalie Mnatalie MmmmmNewport!"

I woke up smiling. I couldn't help it. "Yes, Kiki? How can I help you this morning?"

"Actually you mknow, it's all about mehow *we* can help *you*," Claw said, coming up to me, nuzzling the coffee table leg. Apparently, I had fallen asleep on the couch. I hadn't heard any singing this morning. Maybe they'd done their rehearsing in the middle of the night.

"I'm all ears," I said.

"You mneed to chill," he continued. "As in mmmrow,…take Jin's adviccccce."

"So you're telling me to relax. Why, exactly?"

"Becausssse, all informationsss will mmmmeow….come to you in due time," Kiki answered. "Your sssister…she doesssn't know you're seeking her…mrow, but she has a type of intuitionnn about thingsss. She sssensesss sssomething is about to happennn."

"Jinnn will help you find her," Claw said. "You don't have to sssolve everything yoursssselfff."

"Well thank you both, I appreciate it."

"Oh and alssso. For Christmasss you should sssspice it up for Hammer," Claw said. "Give him a presssent he'll never forget. From a mannn'sss perssspective, thisss is what he wantsss."

"Spice it up? Well he's been here a time or two," I said, waving my hand over myself to indicate where 'here' meant.

"You should danccce for him."

"Oh! I…okay," I said. I giggled at the thought of it, and then asked them what they wanted for Christmas. Kiki answered that she wanted a disssh of whipped creammmeowww. Claw said he wanted gourmet tuna." I assumed he meant the kind I'd gotten from the

Central Market once for a recipe, which still came in a can but was from Italy, and made a mental note of it.

"That'sss the ssstuff," he stuttered.

I woke myself up still laughing at the various levels at which this conversation had taken place. Life and sister advice, and Christmas gift advice for both Hammer and my cats, who were sitting exactly where they had been a second ago, looking at me. They both looked away nonchalantly the minute I woke up—a very human gesture.

"That was *almost* an admission that we had this conversation," I noted, audibly enough that they could hear me calling them out. They said nothing, but I saw a cat smile form across Claw's face before he turned, walked proudly into the kitchen, and nibbled all too innocently on kitty kibble.

~*~

In the midst of workouts, cookouts, and the occasional stress-based freakout, I told Hammer about my sister.

His main question was why Jin had waited this long to tell me. I couldn't answer that. I couldn't answer a lot of things, these days. But I was determined to figure it all out.

The message I got, however, from Jin and from my all-knowing cats, was to relax. I knew I needed to—could feel that. I decided to take their advice. I decided to hit the gym and instead of training or learning anything or thinking too much like I always did, I'd go swimming. I would frolic and float in the water and just make myself feel better that way. It was so soothing to my soul.

I thought about the general theme of relaxing, and what else fit under that heading. Hmmm…oh! Hammer had bought me a massage, and I hadn't redeemed it. No time. Thankfully, he had gotten the gift certificate for me with a massage therapist at my gym, and she was good. So I called the gym to see if she was available, and by some miracle, she was. I would take the kids to the gym daycare and swim, and then get a massage. And then later I'd maybe fix Hammer and I some Japanese food. I had been learning to make sushi, which we both enjoyed, and a few other side dishes.

I was a girl with a plan. To save time, I teleported to my usual wooded spot behind the gym, to make sure nobody saw me. I always laughed to myself when I passed the fire alarm on the way in, remembering how it all started, with Cameron pulling it that day. Those days were long past though, I thought as I walked on up the stairs to change into my suit. I swam and swam, for about an hour and a half and then met Sage, the massage therapist. She asked me where I hurt and I told her just general tension and stress. She said she always enjoyed working the knots out of me, because she knew I needed it so much and it presented her with a challenge. I had to laugh. "Yeah, I'm a challenge, and also challenged." We giggled and I settled down into the massage bed.

A CD of Asian meditation music played in the background—I recognized the soothing sound of the Shakuhachi, or bamboo flute. She started with my feet, spending a lot of time on them. I needed so much work. My body was so stiff and crackly. I relaxed under her touch, like I hadn't in a long time.

I felt myself drifting over the ocean again. I wasn't flying; my body was still on the massage table. My mind was just wandering. I let it wander.

Maybe this little episode was meant for me to practice landing without actually flying, to be safe, but I didn't land anywhere. I just heard a voice coaxing me to come on back to the massage room when I was ready. But oddly, it wasn't Sage's voice. It was a male voice, again with an accent, but not British. I thought to myself, "Why must I be such a freak of nature? I am always hearing voices and having visions! Can't I just have a relaxing afternoon at the gym?"

I heard soft, throaty laughter coming from this male voice. "Oh Natalie, you are amusing indeed," he said.

"Amusing though I may be, it seems I'm not quite done drifting yet. I...I guess my brain needs a longer break," I said. I was trapped floating over a placid sea, and wondered how to get back to whoever was calling.

More throaty laughter. "It's okay, I'll wait," the voice said.

Well, at least he sounds patient.

Oddly, I seemed to be speeding up in my floating. Like someone was watching me on a DVD and pressing the fast forward x 108 button.

Suddenly, I was inside the sphere with Jin.

"Study this; there will be a quiz later," Jin said in all seriousness, inside my head. I looked in the direction he was gazing, and there was a castle made of stone, surrounded by three moats, all of which were surrounded by the sea. My body started to drift around the perimeter. I focused my eyes on all the turrets and rectangular windows, gauging the width of the moats— each one about fifty feet across, and I estimated about one hundred feet deep. The last moat had a drawbridge. There were four turrets, one on each corner of the castle. They were shaped like giant cylinders, so that each one had a lookout on top—flat, not pointy turrets. The top of the castle was also stone. It was a relatively simple shape, a square with the walls being about three-fourths as high as the turrets.

"Here's where it un-simplifies," Jin said. He stood behind me and put his hands on my head. Suddenly, I was peering with laser vision inside the castle. Inside the castle was another castle! But it was a Japanese castle. The exterior of this structure was an exact replica of Matsumoto Castle, which was built like a giant pagoda.

"Is this your superpower?" I said. "The laser vision?"

"It's one of a few," he replied, nonchalantly and without ego.

I was stunned. Jin's laser vision was truly amazing. I could see everything, down to the minutiae of the inside of the structure. In the center of the Japanese castle was a sunken room with a lavish decorative waterfall in the middle. I studied the layout of all the rooms inside. It was gargantuan.

"Do you think you can commit the layout to memory?"

"Yes," I said, scrutinizing every last detail.

"Okay," Jin said.

And with that, we faced each other again in the sphere.

"Sorry to pull you out of your massage, but I needed to get you when you were fully relaxed, so you could be 100% focused on the task."

"It's okay," I said, still somewhat shell shocked. "Now I know why you urged me to relax," I said chuckling. "It's all so clear to me now."

I heard Jin respond by laughing in admittance, and just like that, I was back on the massage table.

*You mustn't be afraid
to dream a little bigger, darling.*

**Tom Hardy
Inception**

Chapter 16

After my massage, I hit the steam sauna for the full and complete detox experience. There wasn't anyone else in it, as classes had ended and there would be at least a 10 minute lull between them before the next flock of women came bounding in to the locker room. I took a deep breath and a sip of bottled water, and lay down on a bunch of towels as the place steamed up fully. The infused scent of peppermint was relaxing and invigorating all at the same time. Suddenly, I heard breathing, kitty corner from me. Strange, I hadn't heard the door open.

"Hello?" I said.

"Hello, I'm here. How are you?" a male voice inquired.

"Well currently, naked, but I'm in a towel so I guess we can talk. Who are you?" I was beyond being surprised at this point.

"Oh, it doesn't matter so much who I am," he said, chuckling. I was too rattled from the events of the day to argue. "I'm simply here to tell you that you're capable of doing great things for the planet."

"That's wonderful," I said.

"Yes, it really is. I know you worry about money and helping Hammer out, but you really needn't. Your destiny is greater than you could ever imagine, and the rest of what you have to do will unfold in time. In the process, the money thing will take care of itself. You might've already heard this from your Sifu or others, but sometimes it takes…repetition…to really sink in," he concluded.

"Thank you," I said. "I have heard a similar message from Jin, yes, but not exactly the same. Not about the financial aspect of things," I said, struggling to identify the man behind this familiar voice.

"Just follow the path you've found, and all of the details will work themselves out in time," he said. "The universe has a way of fine tuning things, beyond what we think it is capable of, or can understand. Also, Hammer earns enough money to support you while you figure things out, and he enjoys doing so. He is a true provider and very much a giver. So let him provide, and give."

I found my mind wandering to my family, and wondering if I was on so-called Pagoda time right now, or if time was elapsing at normal speeds. And if they were waiting for me, because I felt I was heading towards having been there a couple hours at this point.

"Again with the anxiety, Natalie!" the voice said, laughing. "Calm yourself, lass. You are indeed on Pagoda time right now. When you leave this room, an hour plus the time it takes you to get dressed will have passed, and not a minute more."

I took a deep breath and relaxed, again, or tried to.

"Okay. Is there more?"

"One more thing: your sister. She needs you just as much as you need her. The way to find her is, to go to the...I believe you refer to it as the sphere. From there, use the force," he said. "You will be guided somewhat by Jin and Hunter, but you must find her yourself, in the end."

"You know them?"

"Yes, I do."

And then he was gone.

And I realized I had just been talking to the international singing sensation and celebrity champion of many global causes known as Bono, from U2.

~*~

"Okay, so let me get this straight," Sam said. I was really glad we had unlimited after-hours minutes. "Your cats not only talk now but *sing*, you have not only a sister but an identical *twin* sister, you need to find her, you were advised to stop worrying about finances, you will have help when needed, and in the past two weeks you've met both Sting *and* Bono?" Sam was so efficient at processing quickly and summing things up.

"In a word, yes."

"Curiouser and curiouser."

"Indeed," I said.

"So you're going to need help," she concluded.

"It is decidedly so."

Sam laughed. "Ah, the wise words of the Magic Eight-ball."

"Yes," I said. "I've been playing with it since we got on the phone." I heard Sam giggle with familiarity. When we first met, she'd been buying prizes for a contest they were having at the bank she worked at, and I had driven by to see her and won the Magic Eight-ball.

"How are the twins?"

"They're doing great," I said, watching them and smiling. "They're so well-behaved, this far."

"Ah, your karma for having dealt with the toddlers from hell," Sam said. I could hear the smirk in her voice. She had never liked that I'd taken that nanny job. I guess she saw through the parents right away; unfortunately it had taken me a while longer.

"Yeah, I hope it lasts. They'll be teething soon, so that'll be an adventure. They are so wonderful, though. I know I didn't exactly plan it, and it happened sooner than I would have liked, I wouldn't trade this for anything. Speaking of kids…" I said, opening the door on this topic for Sam to step through.

"Actually, we've been trying. Or, not trying really. Just not *not* trying. We haven't been using any birth control for several months now. So, can you look into your crystal ball and tell me if it's in the cards for us? I'd like to know. You know I've always wanted kids," she said wistfully.

I shook the Magic Eight-ball, hoping it had the right answer. She'd know if I were bluffing. "You may rely on it."

Sam laughed with delight. Sometimes all it took was a ray of hope from the tiniest thing to restore one's faith in the future. I was glad to be the instrument for that, today. Or be holding it in my hands. "Gotta love the Magic Eight-ball," I said with a smile that I knew she couldn't see but could hear, and she agreed. She said to let her know if I needed her assistance with the unsolved mystery of my life, and I said I would, even at two a.m. because I knew she was a night owl, and we hung up.

I didn't say goodbye; I tried to never use that word, so I said "See you soon" and quietly put down the phone. I knew I couldn't control it, but that didn't stop me from not wanting any more goodbyes in my life.

I was so thankful to Jin for telling me to relax. Not to mention thankful to my cats, for furthering the message—crazy as that would sound to anyone not knowing the context. I could now focus on the task I'd been given, the only one with any concreteness thus far: finding my sister.

After some assorted kid and cat and cleaning duties, the couch looked inviting so I grabbed a book and sunk into it. Shortly after closing my eyes, I was in a giant funnel spinning downward in a spiral I couldn't get out of. It spit me out the other end and I landed in a dark tunnel. I could see a tiny light so began running towards it while feeling the walls to keep steady. I ran and ran for what seemed like miles, finally reaching the light.

When I came out the other end, I froze and then awoke suddenly with the knowledge that Nozomi now knew about me, because she was standing at the other end of this tunnel! I awoke just before getting to her, but she had looked shocked and then smiled in recognition right before I could reach out and hug her. It felt so real! Unfortunately so did the perspiration from running in my dream, so I got up and hit the shower, deep in thought about my next move.

Teachers open the door,
but you must enter by
yourself.

Chinese Proverb

Chapter 17

I needed to find Nozomi as soon as I could, and to search my soul for answers, so beamed myself to the pagoda. Since I had my own suite of rooms there, I asked Jade to watch the kids during my stay. She answered my unspoken question about being allowed to take them along with me there by saying I could, but not just yet. That seemed to be the answer to a lot of things these days, and I just had to be content with it for now. I thought it would be a place I could protect them, but maybe there were rules I didn't know about.

I kissed the kids and hugged Jade, who seemed okay with that gesture judging by the smile on her face when I left. Since she didn't have children, she was all too happy to watch mine when I needed.

Moments after arriving at the pagoda, I made my way through the forest to the sandy beach. I gazed out at the waves, wondering which part of the ocean my dear, long lost sister could be sailing at this moment, and where she was heading.

"My mind's racing, from chasing pirates..." The Norah Jones song echoed in my ears. I laughed, thinking how crazy this all was and how my life differed from a couple years before, pre-and post superhero status. I still felt very much like a superhero-in-training.

"Well, in a sense, you are," Jin said, suddenly standing beside me, smiling.

"Oh! Hello! Must you always sneak up on me like that?" I laughed and welcomed him with a hug. I was determined to change this cultural formality to something less formal. At least outside the training studio.

"Sorry. Just trying to keep you on your toes," he said with a grin.

"You have inside you, a map," Jin said, getting right down to business. "An internal map and compass to guide you to those who need you. It is the same one you have used to summon those you've needed in times of danger or distress, or simply to learn lessons. You can access it now as a map that you can literally see. The map in the sphere was actually inside you, you just didn't know it at the time."

Interesting, I thought. I couldn't exactly unfold a map from inside myself. Guess I'd have to close my eyes and visualize.

"Exactly," Jin said. "Just picture the one in the sphere. See it how it was when we looked at it that day. I have to go now. Good luck," he said, giving my hand a squeeze. And he was gone.

"Thank you," I said, bowing my head with my hands in prayer position. I gazed out at the water, and then closed my eyes, hands on temples, working on visualizing this map and compass. I brought it into my consciousness, seeing the earth from afar. It was on a map, rotating ever so slowly. I honed in on the oceans, seeing North and South Pacific, North and South Atlantic, the Indian and the Arctic, and all of the seas. Having spent the good majority of my life on land, I had very little idea where modern-day buccaneers hung out, and even less of an idea where one might find my sister, the good pirate Nozomi. So I decided to have a closer look.

I closed my eyes and the map was in front of me. When I opened them it was still there, surrounding me. I was in my own little map bubble. After about twenty real-time minutes of scanning for clues to here whereabouts with little success, I suddenly felt a wave of tiredness. *Maybe a little New York's finest coffee would be in order at such a moment.*

Suddenly, I stood outside that very same NYC coffee shop, feeling the breeze and the bustle of the city. I smiled to be back here, among the unfamiliar, and yet...

Walking in to Mr. Java, I was greeted by Hunter's smiling, mischievous face. "Miss Natalie, I presume," he said, handing me a sixteen-ounce version of my drink. "Triple shot, for extra brain boosting power," he said. I thanked him.

"It really is all about balance, isn't it?" I said. "Work and play, health drinks and caffeinated ones..." I trailed off.

"Indeed. I've been expecting you."

"Have you?"

"Well, I had a feeling," was his response. I had a feeling he knew a lot more than he was telling me.

"Yes. So you know why I've come?" I challenged.

"You needed a brain boost for finding your sister. You thought you might be able to access the sphere more clearly after the caffeine jolt, and also, from here. You are most welcome to try," he said.

I thanked him and proceeded through the doors and hallways to where we accessed it before. It was easier to access the whole earth visual, here. Sitting down to meditate on finding her and finish my coffee, I took a seat on the floor, closed my eyes and put my back against the wall. I heard a voice yelling for me. "Find me, Natalie! I need you!"

The plea sounded urgent. I knew it was her. Unlike when I rescued the family from the fire, this caught in my heart. It had a very personal ring to it.

"Where are you, Nozomi?"

I waited, but no answer. I needed clues. I remembered Sting's words about having help if I needed it. I didn't even know who to ask this time, and looking at the whole world, seeing so many seaports to choose from, was overwhelming. I had no frame of reference, and wasn't about to get started without it or wander aimlessly. I thought about where any clues could be hidden. I couldn't just Google search her, and I didn't feel comfortable asking pirates if they knew or knew of her, either. Most pirates I'd hear of weren't exactly known for their helpfulness.

A blinking light presented itself in the middle of the sphere, so I moved toward it. Zooming in, I saw that it belonged to a lighthouse that was striped like a candy cane, white with a long red swirl up the sides, but couldn't tell if it was occupied or not. Then the sphere went dark. Blank. And on the opposite end of the room from where I'd come in, a sort of door appeared. More of a portal. It looked like the universe was inside, alive with a myriad of colors—purples, blues, greens, with some silver and gold sprinkles thrown in. Whatever was going on in there looked like a party. I surmised that I was supposed to walk through this enchanted door, and that if I did, I wouldn't be trapped like Carol Anne was by the TV People in *Poltergeist*. I didn't hear a voice telling me not to go into the light. For once, I heard no voices at all, American or otherwise.

I stepped through, and was vacuum-sucked instantly through what seemed like a huge tube—much like going down an enclosed waterslide, but without the curves, thankfully. It was very fast and slightly scary, only lasted about twenty seconds, and then out of the blue, green and purple I was thrust out of the waterslide-like ride and onto the ground in front of the lighthouse door. Ouch! I hoped that we could try for a cushioned landing next time.

Lighthouses
don't go running all over an island
looking for boats to save;
they just stand there
shining.

Anne Lamott

Chapter 18

The door to this candy cane style lighthouse creaked open by itself into what looked like the main level of the lighthouse. I deduced it was the main level because before me, a gigantic spiral staircase shot up into the heavens.

Hmm, stairs. Hmm, teleporting? I tried it, but teleporting to the top wasn't the order of the day.

Gonna make me work for it, huh? I laughed to myself as I got my thorough thigh workout for the day. Decades later, I arrived at a giant doorway with a big metal knocker. Listening for sounds on the other side of that door, I heard none. Rap, rap, rap.

I peered in and stepped inside the room, which was unlit except for by two lighthouse windows—darker than I'd expected, for a lighthouse. A man stood on the far side of the room. He had a long grey beard and piercing blue eyes, one open more than the other, giving him a permanent squint.

"I've been expecting you," he said, a big wooden pipe hanging out the corner of his mouth. I smelled the strong scent of not just any vanilla. This was vanilla cake frosting, and I could taste it on my tongue as I breathed in! The scent was intoxicating!

I surmised that no introductions were necessary, since he'd apparently already known I'd be visiting today.

Surveying the scene, his table was filled with maps, nautical charts, and many other objects I knew not the nature of. He clicked on a light so I could see what he was doing. "Donovan," he said rather proudly in an Irish brogue, sticking out his hand. "Donovan the Dude."

"Natalie. Nice to meet you," I said by way of reply.

"Ready to find this sister of yours?"

"Yes. She called me to find her earlier. I had and still have no idea where to begin." I wondered if we were still on Pagoda time or if not, if we had to hurry.

"We're still on Pagoda time," he said. *Ah, so he **was** another guide who could read my thoughts.* "Also, that's why you were brought, or rather hurled through time and space, here. I'll be your captain for what should be quite a voyage indeed. Perhaps, even the voyage of a lifetime," he said, snorting and cackling. He had an endearing, infectious laugh so I found myself laughing along too. It might have also been the vanilla tobacco, affecting my brain cells. And then I snapped back into reality.

Oh, wow. So I should've stopped by my arsenal to get some weapons and clothing, I thought.

"Actually, Jade packed for you. Your bag is on the boat."

"Okay…thanks Jade. Where's the boat?"

"We'll go there in a few, I just have to finish up here." I went to the other side of his table and gaped at all the instruments. Beside them, there was a box.

"That's for you," he said.

Wow, a gift, so soon? We just met.

I took the black, palm-sized box, which was heavier than I thought, and opened it. Inside was a large compass. It was silver rimmed with a gold interior, and looked fairly normal on the outside, but when I opened it, the thing started spinning and sputtering and whirring wildly, taking on a life of its own and almost jumping out of my hands.

"Wow!"

Donovan laughed. "That's Charlie," he said. I had entered the land where every inanimate object also had a name. I liked it here. Charlie was dancing in my hand, ready to get a move on. "He'll help us find Nozomi," Donovan said. Apparently, Charlie could hear because when Donovan said that, he went wild, doing an Irish jig with music to match.

"He's an animated little feller," Donovan said.

"I noticed!"

"Oh, and I meant to tell you, the reason it's so dark in here is that we're not on the top deck. If you continue up the staircase, you can see it." This was an invitation out of his man-cave-space, I surmised, rather amused. So out of the room and up I went. The 360-degree view was amazing. I walked all the way around, sending a mental message to Nozomi, out over the oceans, that I was coming for her. I could use Sam's company right now, but she was probably busy. Wow, would I have a lot to tell her when the time was right.

I looked down expecting to see a large vessel, and saw what must have been "the boat" that Donovan was referring to. It was…well, for lack of a better word, a clunker. I saw the name *Calliope* painted on the stern and wondered if that was as in, the Greek goddess, or the instrument? Interesting.

He appeared in the doorway. "We're going out onto the open ocean…in *that*?" I asked, thinking this would surely have a *Perfect Storm* type of ending.

"Just you wait, lassie," was his cackling response. "You'll see."

We boarded the boat in relative silence. Donovan showed me to my quarters, which consisted of a little cabin, separated from the main part of the boat by a few stairs and a curtain, with raised twin beds. I hoisted myself up onto the one without the bag. He told me to rest, that I'd need it, and I wasted no time in going to that place.

I awoke sometime later with a bunch of questions in my head, and Jin sitting across from me. "Oh!" said I, startled enough to sit up quickly and hit my head on the low ceiling. Luckily, I didn't thump it hard enough to knock me out or anything.

He chuckled. "Lie down and relax, Phoenix," he said. "I'm going to look within at what questions you have and answer them so you don't have to ask this time."

What a relief. I had a million and a half questions.

"The reason you can't teleport to your sister like you did to the family in the fire is because the pirates she sails with are equipped with more power than humans have. They have taken her hostage, because they've turned to greed and destruction. It doesn't take long for this to happen in the world, and more specifically, *her* world. Much like you're a force for good, so is she—but amongst a cluster of corrupt seafaring men. They know you're coming and they're 'blocking' you from seeing her. She was the captain of the ship, but her crew has taken it over and they're taking shifts being captain, and in questioning her as well.

"Since she was born, she's had a life purpose that she didn't know until recently. Hers is intertwined with yours. She knows secrets that no one else does. Her crew thinks she knows where a treasure is hidden, and she does, but the kind she protects is not the sort of treasure they seek. They are only keeping her for this purpose. They don't care about lives that don't matter to them—meaning, the lives that can't help make them richer. They are truly the terrorists of the ocean, now.

"When they started out, Nozomi sailed a ship that was one of a kind. Her gang was more one of caretakers and cleaners. They would only salvage needed supplies from ships that had already been abandoned, leaving everything else including the ocean itself much better than they'd found it. They would take any bits of treasure from those ships, but only enough to survive on, and machinery, enough to repair their own boat when necessary. They were a team, and they worked as a fast, efficient machine, and at times, as a patrol ship disguised as a pirate ship, making sure things didn't get out of control.

"Somewhere along the way, one of her pirates, the one who was lazy and a bit shifty to begin with but who they took on needing one more man, began to think about how much easier it was to live a dishonest life, planting it like a seed at first with one and then it began to spread this among his shipmates like a rampant weed. It grew out of control until it took over the ship and these formerly good men. Nozomi was the only one strong enough not to be taken over by this way of thinking.

"Your sister doesn't have the ability to teleport like you do; she has other powers—powers of sight. This means all travel, all of her life since her teens, has been done by water. She's been on the water for many years. This means she doesn't have land legs anymore, so she will be unsteady at first when she tries to walk on land again. It's going to be challenging, because you need her help with your mission. But you'll be able to make good use of Pagoda time."

He paused, reading my further questions.

"No, she isn't so far away that we have a huge journey."

Finally, we were getting down to brass tacks. Something in me needed to know *where* on the planet my sister was. I just couldn't quite get comfortable going to an unknown destination, so if there was a way to find out, I would.

"I will tell you where we're going, but I can only tell you so much. Your sister has sailed the world, but was making her way to you when her crew turned to the Dark Side. She was sailing to this region of the world, without even knowing why. She was following her intuition, and her homing instinct. Her heart knew it was searching for something. She has been navigating towards it for about a year now. Towards you. Your heart is the treasure she seeks," he finished.

Donovan interrupted from the deck. "You might need to strap in," he said.

Strap in? What happened to simple life jackets?

I heard him cackle again in response. Hmmm...what was I getting myself into here? I barely had time to go down that thought path, as Jin had taken my hand and was leading me up the stairs.

Our ideals resemble the stars,
which illuminate the night.
No one will ever be able to touch them. But
the men who,
like the sailors on the ocean,
take them for guides,
will undoubtedly
reach their goal.

Carl Schurz

Chapter 19

So there we were: me, with the core of my body strapped in snugly to a Space Age chair of awesomeness; Donovan at the wheel, in a standing-version of what I was sitting in, and Jin, kneeling in front of me, giving instructions. I was listening to him, while enjoying this ergonomically correct chair and its lumbar support. How relaxing for this tumultuous trip!

"Okay, Phoenix. The ride is going to be a bit shaky, but you'll be fine. If something should happen mid-voyage, use Charlie. Charlie is your own personal compass and will guide you once you reach where you're going, because Donovan has to stay aboard and guard the boat."

I thought it odd that Jin had said the word "shaky" instead of "rough" or something similar. The time for instructions had passed, apparently, because there was indeed some serious shaky stuff going on with this boat. Jin leaned over, kissed my cheek, whispered something in my ear, and then disappeared.

All I could do, strapped in like this—besides operate Charlie, which I didn't really know how to do—was observe. What I observed was incredible. It was like the boat was being shrink-wrapped from the outside, in some substance that looked a lot like purple tinfoil, only it wasn't foil at all. It covered the entire boat except for the porthole-style windows on the sides, of which there were four.

"It's a protective sealant," Donovan said as we sank rapidly underneath the ocean surface. My ears started to pop.

As promised, the whole kit-and-caboodle started to shake, rattle and roll as we made our descent into the depths. I figured now that the name of this vessel had to do with the sound she made: *Calliope*'s cacophony. I could feel my brain vibrating against my skull! I was glad I hadn't eaten yet, as I surely would've upchucked. This sinking lasted for roughly thirty real-time minutes, and then abruptly stopped. Where was the Dramamine when we needed it?

Donovan turned his head as far as he could in my direction, and asked if I was okay. I gathered my wits and came to my senses as much as possible, but a simple "I think so" was all I could muster. My voice didn't sound like my own. It sounded like I'd sucked some helium from a balloon, and so did Donovan's. Therefore, I got the giggles. And so did Donovan. We laughed for a good few minutes, and our laughs were high-pitched also, which sent us further and further into gales of laughter.

This laugh-a-thon finally subsided and I felt could speak again. "I needed that," I said.

Donovan grinned at me, eyes of mischief sparkling. "I should probably explain why we are 20,000 leagues under the sea."

"I'm all ears."

"Your sister is being held captive in the harbor of a secret island—one that doesn't exist on maps. People who aren't invited there don't know about it, and those who find out aren't welcome. The island's inhabitants like to keep the place a secret. It's so beautiful and pristine and it would be a supreme vacation destination, but resorts and the like would be shunned by those who have lived there for years. They feel the world has enough of those already, and as much of a money maker it would be, such a venture would waste the resources and completely change the energy of the island."

I let this sink in for a moment. I didn't think there were still places even cartographers didn't know about, or were sworn to secrecy about.

"So we had to turn 'ol *Calliope* into a submarine. The process wasn't easy, but we did it. This was literally the only way we could get here. Also, the quickest—if we're measuring on real time, which actually does matter somewhat in this instance, because the pirates will eventually leave. As far as we could guesstimate, they are planning on staying 'til tomorrow, but who knows, with these guys."

"Will I be able to see them? As in, their locations onboard, before I go?

"I don't think so. They're blocking anyone from seeing anything. You have to be actually aboard ship to know what's going on," he replied. *Great.*

"By the way, I know *Calliope* doesn't look like much on the outside, but that's on purpose. Wouldn't want anyone knowing what she's got on the inside," he explained, grinning at all the gadgets and gizmos that surrounded him and giving the boat a pat. "Right now, we're doing the equivalent of treading water, staying in one place. She can't hold down here much longer, so I'll tell you what I know about what you have to do, and then we'll be up, up and away."

"We'll emerge around the corner from Nozomi's ship, which is easy to spot amongst the others at the harbor, because of the flag. It's black in background, and has her name and likeness on it. You'll know what to do from there." I started to prep myself at my usual pace, racing down the stairs to get my bag, and saw that there was a stash of protein bars in the side pocket, so grabbed one and started eating it. Donovan caught me as I was running back up the stairs, and said "Remember, you're on Pagoda time, so this mission doesn't require a rush job. Slow and steady, Phoenix."

"Thanks," I said, wondering how I'd do slow and steady with this rush of adrenaline running through my veins.

It's never too late to get
what you need...
sometimes you just gotta
go ahead and
ask for it...
the universe is listening.

Glenn Hughes

Chapter 20

The process of rising to the surface was a bit less painful than the sinking had been. I felt like an old pro by now, but my stomach was still queasy. When we got there, the covering on the boat disappeared, or…dissolved, it looked like. I centered myself and stabilized my energy before looking around. It was a beautiful island from what I could see, but we weren't here to sightsee.

I spotted the ship, which was charcoal grey and attractive—especially so among the many eyesores. It was very much a woman's ship, and a classy woman at that, as this ship was, for lack of a better word, accessorized. The charcoal of the boat was set off by the trim which was black, finished off with silver tips, all the way around. The flag itself matched the ship—charcoal, then black, and silver on the very edge. As Donovan had mentioned, Nozomi's face was superimposed on the flag—she was smiling and holding a rose in her teeth—a rose that went from deep burgundy at the bottom to pale pink at the tip. Nozomi was all about the details. I honed in on where she was, inside, but my super secret stealth skills weren't working. The crew was truly blocking her from being seen.

Charlie started jumping around in my hand, and I reached down and put him on silent, though a second ago I hadn't known how to do that; it seemed I'd been infused with the knowledge of how to work him. "Sorry, I can't control it sometimes. I was designed to dance around. You'll still be able to hear me, Natalie," he said, in a very echo-chamber type of voice.

"Thanks Charlie," I said. It was all I could think of to say at the time. My mind was blown that he actually spoke, too, but I wasn't going to allow myself to get sidetracked. I tweaked his settings and pulled up his antennae.

"Ah, thanks, it's been a while," he said. I swear I could hear him popping and cracking with relief, just like a human with bones. I giggled at how relieved he sounded. I knew we were in a serious moment, but my nerves were fairly frazzled and I needed some brevity to balance that out, so I told him chiropractic adjustments were free. It was nice to have a friend to go into this with. This was weird, but seriously cool because it meant I wasn't totally alone.

I clipped Charlie to my side and grabbed the backpack, which I'd just spotted inside the bigger bag Jade had packed. She'd thought of everything. It contained some more foodstuffs for Nozomi and some incidentals—i.e. mini-ninja stars. I had changed my clothes, too. Or, they had been changed for me actually. I was wearing all black, in a material I had never experienced. It wasn't leather but much lighter and breathable, but still kept me insulated. I had a scarf exactly like Nozomi's flag but without her face, just the rose, tied around my head, pirate-style, and a sword hitched on the other side of me than Charlie was—good thing Jin had taught me sword fighting. Couldn't be sure, but I had an inkling that everything in the backpack would be exactly what I needed. This was good, as I didn't (and apparently couldn't) know what I was up against.

Donovan wished me luck, and off I went. I beamed myself from our boat onto theirs.

~*~

I barely had two seconds to do my Sherlock Scan of the top deck. There were only two pirates here. One was actually swabbing the deck, and the other was in a chair mumbling to himself—drunk. Number Two would be easy, but the deck swabber was buff, bald, and a brute—could've easily been a bodyguard or a bouncer. He turned towards me and I tried to disappear and reappear behind him but it didn't work. Time to rely on the fighting skills!

He came at me and I felt him summing me up, looking for weak points. I didn't think he'd find many, but would probably assume I had a weak stomach and go for that. What he didn't know was, I was summing him up at the same time, and here's what I came up with: all brawn, no brains! So I just had to deal with those few brain cells he did have in his biceps.

I reached down into my backpack and found something I hadn't seen there before: a big cast iron skillet! Knowing immediately what to do with this, I let this big oaf come at me, and conked him on the head with all the force I could muster. He stood there like a cartoon with little birds tweeting around his head, his eyes losing focus, and finally teetered to a fall. "Timber!" I shouted.

Charlie laughed. The drunken pirate belched loudly and said "Scuze me," and I got to work tying up the big guy. I looked over my shoulder, surprised the thud of his fall hadn't attracted any attention, but maybe the others were being loud themselves. While I was tying him up, the drunken one had gotten up from where he'd sat and staggered toward me. He stopped singing "Yo ho ho and a bottle of rum" and began bellowing "Avast! Belay there with the fightin', you're a lass and ye'll never win!" He paused to burp once again and continued, "Ya scurvy dogs below decks! Thar be a beauty onboard who resembles our captain, but she's a lily livered landlubber!" He slipped on the still-wet deck and fell on his bum with a crash, and then started crawling in my direction.

I looked into my magical backpack, where there appeared a bottle of rum. Yo ho ho. This guy was too far gone to be belligerent. He reached out to grab the bottle from my hand, and I had him by the wrist, which I pulled down to the railing and tied, fastening it to his other wrist and both feet. He was now, for all intents and purposes, a part of the ship's structure, and he wasn't protesting because he had a new bottle of rum. I tied his left ankle to the brute's right ankle. Two down, two and possibly three to go!

I was, however, worried about the others I had to take down. "Charlie, I still can't see where the rest are or where Nozomi is. Can you assist?"

He started beeping wildly at my side like R2D2, and said, "There is one directly below us on the landing of the stairs." Fighting on a landing would prove difficult, so I decided to get his attention and bring him up on deck. I ran down the narrow stairs and said "Boo! Catch me if you can!" and then turned on my heel and ran back up. He was right on my tail. This one was athletic and smart, more of a match for me and a threat. But *he* didn't have a magic backpack. With mine plus Charlie, I was a triple threat! I reached in and pulled out a small bag of flour, ripping it open and throwing it in his eyes. He exclaimed and it slowed him down some, but he pulled out his sword a minute later and charged at me with it.

For some reason, I looked in the backpack instead of pulling out my sword immediately. A red scarf! I pulled out the scarf and said "Toro, toro!" and he sliced it in half with his sword as he ran, but he was charging so hard he couldn't stop, so he ran all the way to the back of the ship, hitting the railing in his stomach and knocking the wind out of himself. Charlie, still at my side, continued to howl with delight. This was a lot like fighting cartoon pirates who tripped over their own feet, but this pirate had an aura of evil around him. If I wouldn't have been so amped on adrenaline, I'd have been scared.

I pulled out my sword and awaited the man's advance. He did so more cautiously this time, and we began to spar. Ninja meets pirate at last. I was keeping up with him well even though sword fighting was not my specialty. "Arrr, I'll get ye, me beauty!" threatened the one I was fighting. Clink, clink, clink went the swords! "Oooh, ouch, ahh!" exclaimed Charlie as he got jostled around in the fight, and the drunken one was cheering on his shipmate with slurred shouts that couldn't be made out.

My opponent seemed happy to keep up this dance for a while, but I was not, so I sped up my sparring, attempting to get his sword out of his hands and pin him to the ground. Alas, this plan was not to be, as another pirate came bellowing up the stairs. This was number four. "Ahoy there, darlin'!" he said, drawing his sword, and suddenly I was fighting two at once. I wondered if I could mess with their mojo enough to turn them against each other. Not likely, as they were both smarter than the dunderhead I had first fought. "Backpack, Natalie!" Charlie said in the excited echo-ey whisper of someone who was watching a fight but didn't want to intrude.

I tried to disappear but my powers were still useless here, so I held them off for a moment using all my strength. Unfortunately, all my strength wasn't enough. One of them got his sword all the way to me. I harnessed everything I could, from the lesson at the waterfall trying to make myself impenetrable. But it was not enough. He was too quick, and the dark magic was too strong on this ship.

Charlie took one for the team, jumping directly in front of the sword's tip! Pingggg! The jab would've run me through, to be sure, if it weren't for this little compass with the big personality. I looked down quickly to see if he was okay. He had spun his body backwards, compass end facing me, so it was metal on metal, no damage. "Not even a scratch, Natalie!" he exclaimed with pride. But his voice was a little shaky. I whispered a quick but fervent "thanks" to him, and remembered that I should see what I had to pull out for my next trick. I peeked into the pack. What I saw just about blew my mind.

The greatest treasures are those
invisible to the eye
but found by the
heart.

Anonymous

Chapter 21

Luckily, the scamp and the scoundrel in front of me were tired from fighting harder than usual, and also were interested—more like mesmerized—about what was in my magic backpack, probably hoping it contained treasure or at least a map to it. They just stood, swords again poised against my own in a deadlock, staring at the pack and awaiting their fate. Knowing I needed a few extra seconds, I used all my force and pushed their swords off mine. They lost balance and stumbled around, buying me the needed time.

I couldn't tell what it was at first, but it looked like a crystallized ninja star, intricate with detail. I plucked it perhaps too quickly out of the pack, but it didn't cut me. Instead, it stung my hand with piercing cold. "Ouch!" I said, wishing I were impervious to cold the way I was to heat. "Lasts twenty-five minutes," said an attached tag.

"Fling it, Natalie, fling it!" Charlie squealed with barely concealed delight.

I ripped the tag off with my teeth and threw the star towards the pirates. It nearly reached them, acted like it'd hit an invisible wall, and then rose directly about four feet above them and paused, horizontal like a plate. There, the star started spinning wildly, creating an ice storm to end all ice storms! It was actually a combination of ice, snow and hail, which all spiraled out from the ninja star, quickly covering the pirates and the surface of the boat. They couldn't see each other, much less me! It was the Perfect Storm. ☺

~*~

I reached into the backpack for more rope. I wondered how I'd tie these two up without slipping and sliding all over the place in this ice, but looked down and found I had snow boots on, with incredible traction. I tried not to get distracted by how cute they were—the boots, not the pirates—they were fully water-and-weather-proof with rubber soles, but had a fur lining around the top. Functional *and* fashionable! Plus, it was so nice that I didn't have to change shoes. When Sting, or rather Gordon, said I'd have help, he wasn't kidding. But I digress...

Unhitching Charlie from my side, I saw that he could sort of float in the air, so he could really help me after all! I made a knot and hitched one end of it onto his handle, and directed him to stay put. He said he would, and I didn't listen to anything else because he made me giggle with his antics, so I ran quickly around where I could hear the two sliding and grunting. Charlie helped by twirling himself around and around to deepen the knot. "Thanks Charlie!" I said, doing a light but pointed jog towards the stairs—not enough deck space for a full-on run. I could see clearly and with these boots, could navigate the ice just fine. Ah, the miracle of being a well-dressed superheroine—but today, as a pirate, with modern boots. God, I loved my job.

I ran down the stairs shouting Nozomi's name, and heard a faint gurgle in the cabin to the left, so I turned and saw her—my twin sister, for the first time in roughly fifteen years. Instantly, our childhood together came back to me, the five years we shared before we were separated. I remembered everything: playing by the water and in the woods, the two Christmases we had together that I was old enough to recall, and loving her more than life itself. It was a whirlwind memory playback. I rushed to her, untying and ungagging her.

"Oh, Natalie." Those two words encompassed relief, gratitude, and told me she'd been waiting there like that for a while. She looked emaciated and dehydrated, so I pulled a bottle of water out of the pack and watched her drink like she had never tasted water before. She had scars on her face from being slapped, and a black eye. I was instantly angry that anyone would dare mess with my sister, but there was no time to punch a bag or a pirate right now so I just channeled it into fuel for my mission.

I saw no blood anywhere on her, so I pulled her up to standing, supporting her with my body weight and guiding her up the stairs. "We have to move quickly, Nozomi. I'll help you," I said. She merely nodded in dazed understanding. It was all she could do. I didn't trust these pirates one bit, not even the dimmest of the bulbs among them.

I put her on my back for the trip up the stairs, and when we reached the top I set her down, threw her arm around my shoulder and pulled her to my side. She had a death grip on me, so I knew she knew what was happening. "Don't worry, they're all restrained," I reassured, and she grunted in response. The ice storm was dissipating. I went to the spot where I'd left Charlie and grabbed him.

He was shaking and trying to say something and stuttering. He seemed really scared. "What's that, Charlie?" I asked, trying to get it out of him and making sure the naughty pirates were all still in place.

"N-n-n-nuuuuuuh…"

"Yes, I'm right here. What is it, little guy? We are in a real hurry so please say what's on your mind! Use your words!"

At that point, I heard him gulp and inhale and he found his words. "Natalieeeeeee, behind you! *LOOK!*"

I whirled around and saw with horror what he was looking at. The smart pirate was laser-focused on the sky and some sort of electric current was flowing from his hands, which were tied up together at the wrists. But his fingers were pointing at the sky. In the sky, a huge triple tornado came straight at us! Closer and closer it lurked and loomed, the sky darkening into a charcoal grey that matched the grey on Nozomi's ship. Zoiks!

I had no way of communicating with Jin to ask if there was anything else I needed off the ship, but somehow at that point Nozomi found her words. "M-m-my…"

"What do you need, Nozomi?" I asked hurriedly.

"My…cat," she said.

Oh my God. She had a cat somewhere on this vessel. Knowing how I felt about my felines, that was not something I was willing to leave behind. "Where?"

"I d-d-don't know," she said.

"Great," I muttered. "Charlie, I need you!" He was instantly by my side, saying he'd scout the ship and find this feline.

"Name?"

"F-Fluh-Fluffernutter," she said, giving me a weak smile. Though she was still weak, her eyes were twinkling with humor now. This was a good sign. Charlie went off like he had jet packs on his back.

"Come on, Charlie," I silently pleaded as I supported Nozomi and kept her from fainting or falling overboard.

"Got him!" We heard from the stairs. He reappeared, half-dragging the kitty by its collar. I laughed as I saw that it wore an eye patch on one eye. It was a big tabby, grey and black striped, with a white chest and a beige belly that almost dragged on the ground. I could tell by his eyes that he was super-intelligent, and didn't look drugged or injured. So I picked him up, tossed him on my shoulder, and quickly checked the remaining contents of the bag. It was empty at last, except for the mini-ninja stars, so I considered this job done.

The boat was starting to spin into the sea tornado. "Everybody hang on!" I closed my eyes, focused and beamed us off the boat back onto *Calliope*.

Forgive the person and their actions,
never give in to hate,
let it go,
set it free,
and
Karma will take care of
what is meant to be.

Stargazer

Chapter 22

Reappearing in the belly of the beast, I noted that Nozomi had found her voice, because she was asking a ton of questions at a million miles an hour. "What about *The Rose*? What happened to my crew? Where are we?" She asked about ten more in the next ten seconds, which became gibberish and then, promptly, into my arms, she fainted. She felt so light—too light, to be healthy.

I carried her down the stairs and to the other bed, Donovan's voice behind me saying it was probably better this way, because I wouldn't have to explain the trip back under the ocean and back up.

Jin didn't appear, but his voice filled my head. "A job well done, Phoenix. See you on the other side." I hoped that meant I could take Nozomi to the Pagoda. "Yes. She too has rooms awaiting her there." I did a silent cheer, for I was drained and in need of rest as well. My observance of Nozomi told me that she would need days of respite and nourishment, and perhaps to be cocooned in the love of Jin and Jade and the whole Pagoda experience, much as I had been in the beginning. I leaned over and hugged her sleeping body, kissed her cheek, and turned to go up the stairs, almost running into Jin as I parted the curtain.

"Oh! I didn't know you were here!"

"I'm here. I meant I'd see you on the other side of the curtain," he said, chuckling. I laughed along, sort of collapsing into him. A few tears may have leaked out, from being so amped up and scared I wouldn't be able to reach her.

"Congratulations on rescuing your sister. Mission accomplished. Jade will take it from here," Jin said.

"What's to happen to her pirates?"

"Well, Phoenix…they'll go where bad pirates go," Jin said, grinning. I deciphered that he didn't want me to know their sentence.

"Okay, I won't ask questions," I said, returning his smile.

"To tell you the truth, the pirate who summoned the triple tornado couldn't stop it in time after you narrowly escaped. So it swallowed them and…"

"Smashed the boat and everyone on it to smithereens?"

"Precisely."

"Yuck. Well, it's good to know we don't have to deal with them any more, but I'm sure Nozomi will be upset when she finds out."

"She likely will. But there was no getting them back to good. They were lost to the ways of evil, forever."

"I see. Wow."

"The sea will swallow and recycle them…as it does with all its lifeless forms. Since water is your element, you know this already."

"What is Nozomi's element?"

"Earth."

"Ahhh. Of course. We have been living each other's elements, me on land and she on water."

"Yes. She will eventually want to go back to living on water, as it's really all she knows. But first she must help you with your mission."

"I understand. I don't know how long we've been gone, but it feels like days," I observed.

"We've been gone, your time, half a day."

"Wow. That's it? I so love Pagoda time."

"Yes, that's it. I know you want to check on your family, so feel free to go. You'll be able to teleport back now," he said.

"Okay. Just one thing first." I looked down at Charlie, still hitched to my hip. Unhitching him, I said "I suppose I have to leave you here with Donovan, now."

Charlie actually sniffed. He was crying! Oh this was going to be harder than I thought. I'd gotten attached to my little sidekick. "Y-yes Natalie, this is where I live, with D-d-Donovan," he said, a quiver in his already shaky voice. "I'll m-miss you." He erupted into a shuddering, shivering little compass, so I hugged him to my heart, and he let it all out. Guess he'd been a little stressed about the mission too.

"I'll miss you too Charlie. Do you think we'll see each other again?" I asked. He was still heaving from crying so hard. Who knew a compass could have feelings too? "Breathe, Charlie. Breathe," I said, relaxing him and rubbing his back.

His little body started making R2D2-like sounds again. "My calculations tell me that, yes, we shall meet again," he said. "Ahh, I'm so glad you asked me that."

"Okay, good," I said, feeling good about handing him back to Donovan, which I did, giving the old sailor a hug. "How about you? Do I get to see you again, Donovan?"

"Aye, Natalie," he said. "I believe I'll be seeing you again, in the not too distant future," he replied, pipe smoking. I wondered if it was a magical pipe as I'd never seen him light it.

I quickly squeezed his hand. "I can't thank you enough for your help," and then teleported back to my house. No use prolonging goodbyes.

I checked on the kids. Hammer was at work, and Jade was with them but Hammer came home a few minutes after I did. I thanked and hugged Jade, who congratulated me on doing what was necessary to find Nozomi, and left—disappearing on sight, of course. Why use doors, if you don't have to?

Hammer greeted and hugged me. "You found your sister? Wow! Where is she?" he said.

"I did. I met a sailor named Donovan and a compass named Charlie who took me to her in a clunker boat turned submarine named Calliope. It was epic," I said. "Nozomi's's with Jade now at the Pagoda."

"Wow. Did you get to talk to her?"

"Hardly at all, before she fainted. She was completely dehydrated and malnourished, not to mention tortured. I'm sure there will be time," I said, hoping this was true. I needed to know her, and how her life had been. I needed her to know me.

"Babe. You've been through a lot, I can tell." He was always so good at reading me. I loved this.

"And yet, I feel somehow that this is only the beginning," I said, wishing I could see into my own future. Unfortunately, it didn't work that way. It was never that easy.

*There are some things you
learn best in
calm,
and some in
storm.*

Willa Cather

Part Two

Chapter 23

So I had just rescued my sister from a terrible fate. She could've been tortured to death by good-turned-evil pirates, but fortunately she was free, and safe.

Freedom, and safety: two things that meant the most to me. I couldn't wait to really meet her under less dire circumstances than we'd just been through. But for now, I needed Sam, so I called.

"Oh my god, it is *so* good to hear your voice!" she said.

"Likewise, my friend," I said, and asked her how she'd been.

"Not bad," she said, trying to sound nonchalant, but I could tell there was something going on.

"What is it?"

"What's what?" she said.

"Don't be coy with me, young lady!" I joked.

"There's nothing going on with me that you need to know about right now. I want to know your news," she said.

"How do you know I have news?" I countered.

"Give me a little credit for being your friend."

Pause.

"Okay, actually, I...had a dream about it. I dreamed you found your sister," she said. It was like she was trying to convince herself, and me at the same time, that this is how she knew. But my vibe-o-meter was going off the charts. Something was up.

"Really. Okay. Was it a detailed dream?" I was totally fishing, and we both knew it.

"Yes. I saw how you did it. I know about the lighthouse and Donovan and *Calliope* and Charlie and everything!"

"WOW!" There was still something going on I didn't quite understand. Sam hardly ever had detailed dreams; she had disconnected scenes—she dreamed in symbolism. Not since childhood had she dreamed in a linear fashion. Best friends talk about these things, and we had on several occasions. But I was going to let this go—for now, and I told her so.

"So you know the news I was calling to tell you. Well hot diggety dog! That's just swell, thanks for saving me all the work of describing it!" I said.

"Hey, I do what I can," she said.

"Okay, so you're not going to update me on your life, and you know about mine. What's there to talk about?"

"There's always…sports, I guess," she said.

"Yeah, how 'bout those Mariners…"

"They're…improving," I said.

"True," she parried.

Silence.

"So…that went off like an alarm clock on a Sunday morning at the Waltons," she said. We giggled, missing each other and then I heard babies crying in the background, so I told her I'd be in touch again soon, hoping I spoke the truth in saying this. This life just wasn't so simple to balance, and time to chat was sparse. We said "I love you" as we always did, but simultaneously this time, and hung up. I raced to the twins' room. Hammer beat me there, telling me they were fine, just needed feeding. So together, we took care of that. It was another rare, sweet moment. I couldn't get enough of these.

When the babies had had enough, we burped them and took them into the backyard, laying them on a blanket in the grass so they could be in touch with the outdoors. It was a balmy spring day. We usually let them have a few minutes of morning sunshine on days like this, and then moved them under the umbrella.

We sat facing the Zen garden and behind it, the high fence that blocked us from seeing anyone else's property, and vice versa. "I love what we all did with this place," Hammer remarked.

"I'm so glad. And I do too. Would you like something to drink?"

"Sure, I'd love some of that blackberry green tea you made."

Ever the health-conscious one, I laughed to myself as I went to fill his glass with ice. I was reflecting on how very happy I was that I never saw anyone like Mr. Clean in my counter or Aunt Jemima or Mrs. Butterworth having conversations or fights on the table, when I turned and there was Jin, standing behind me, leaning on said counter. I started, and he laughed, having read my thoughts.

"Sorry to startle you, Phoenix," he said.

"No problem. I was totally expecting you to be right behind me," I said, laughing. "Would you like something to drink? I was just getting Hammer a green tea. Iced."

"Actually, I'd love one," he said. "So sorry to interrupt family time, but I have some important information to impart."

"Please, join us," I said, handing him his tea.

He greeted Hammer and the babies gracefully, bending down to touch the twins' fingers, which curled around his own and clamped on. It was like they recognized him.

"How's Nozomi?" I asked.

"She's healing well, with Colin's help. She's been asking about you and we've told her as much as she needs to know—the basics. The details will be up to you to catch her up on," he said. "What I came today to tell you is very important. I'm glad I have you both together for this," he said, taking a deep, solemn breath.

"Natalie, Hammer, you need to keep a close eye on the kids."

"Closer than usual?"

"Yes, because here's the thing. They will soon be in grave danger."

Anyone can hide.
Facing up to things,
working through them,
that's what makes you
strong.

Sarah Dessen

Chapter 24

A sudden shiver went through my body. I didn't know what he was referring to, but I didn't have to. The look on his face said it all. I looked at them, happily crawling around on the blanket, and thought I would wither and die if anything ever happened to one of these precious little life forms. Hammer grabbed my hand and squeezed.

"How so?" Hammer asked. At that moment, Jade appeared beside Jin.

"His name is Shadow Black," Jin continued. "He is so powerful; a true trickster. But there's one caveat: he possesses the mind of a child and therefore the attention span of one as well."

I let this sink in for a second. "So, only a short-term memory then?"

"Yes. He is obsessed with children—not in a sick way but he wants to study them and see how they work. Therefore, he 'collects' them."

At this point, Hammer's phone went off, and my warning bells went off. He answered and I heard him talking about getting called in. He hung up with them, came over to us and said, "This is terrible timing, but I have to go to work. The Bellego House is on fire, and they need all of us. I'm sorry," he finished, kissing me and looking into my eyes with concern. I could tell he was deep in thought because he didn't have his usual happy-go-lucky gait.

"What does he do with them when they grow up?" I wondered aloud, wanting Hammer to hear this before he left.

"He would have to kill them and is evil enough to do so but doesn't want the mess, so he puts a spell on them and they stop growing. He has quite a collection now of 'orphaned' children."

"That's disgusting," Hammer said.

"The missing children epidemic that's been happening lately," I said.

"Yes," Jin said. "It *is* disgusting, and yes, it *is* related to what's been happening across the country in the past few years, increasing in frequency. He has a brilliant criminal mind. So what he does is to create disasters in order to steal these children while the parents are distracted." He went on, reading my mind. "Like the fire when you rescued the child in the basement of the apartment complex. Shadow Black was on his way there. Your attuned senses must have known somehow. He would've claimed the baby and no one would have known as the parents, according to his plan, were to perish in the fire."

It was all coming together in my head. "So now…"

"Now, he is angry with you," Jin said.

Jade spoke up at last. "Your children are in danger. He will come after them. His is a powerful magic, but we will do our best to protect them."

For the second time that day, although it was warm and pleasant outside, a shiver overtook me. I was sweating and shivering and my stomach hurt and my head was pounding. I stared at Jin. "So when we were in the sphere, you couldn't have directed me to another catastrophe? One where Shadow Black was nowhere near and people just randomly needed saving?"

"Unfortunately, Natalie, I am unable to detect his presence. He is just that sneaky. But even if I could, I am not allowed to interfere with your deeper destiny. I can only help you when you ask for it."

I could feel the truth of his words and did not doubt his sincerity. "So I am destined to fight and attempt to defeat this Shadow Black?"

"Yes. Although fighting him might not be all that you need to do."

"Okay. The castle I saw during my massage session…"

"…is where he lives and collects his 'pets.' That's how he refers to them," Jin finished.

"I see." This was disturbing and frightening news, knowing that I'd gotten in the way of his conquest and now he was coming after my children. "So if he comes for my kids, how will he take care of them? They're only babies."

"He is angry with you, so he won't keep your children. He wants to teach you a lesson, so he will seriously hurt and possibly, kill them, if given the chance."

I felt hot tears of rage and fear surge up behind my eyes, but was determined not to fall to pieces. As usually happened, Hammer had to be gone and couldn't support me, so I had to buck up instead of buckle under pressure. So that is precisely what I intended to do now. Right after I at least spoke with my husband.

"How long do I have?"

"Not long, in either earth time or Pagoda time."

"I need to tell Hammer the rest of what you've told me," I said to Jin, emotion stacked high in my throat.

"Yes, Phoenix," he said tenderly.

"I just want to know one thing first." He nodded for me to go ahead. "You and Jade. Are you siblings, or spouses, or…other?"

"We are brother and sister." He continued, reading my thoughts. "Not angels really, but…"

"Superheroes?"

"Well, in a sense. We do have powers that are beyond human. You could call us…spirit protectors."

"How about Hunter?"

"He was a friend of my father's."

Noting his hush-voiced, short answers, I guessed "Is that all you can tell me now?"

"Yes, about your ninja family."

"But there's more about Shadow Black?"

"Yes. There is much information to relay and much to prepare for."

My worries about finances or any of the usual stuff had now been completely wiped out and replaced by concern for my kids. Jin knew instantly and advised me to do what I was thinking, and directly alert Hammer as well as Sam to the full scope of this news. So I did. I got on the line with both in the next half-hour after Jin and Jade had left. The echoed my worried sentiments. The kids were fine, for now, but Hammer and I agreed on implementing new procedures. One of us would always be with them until this was over, or Jin or Jade if and only if either parent couldn't be there for any reason. No more morning babysitter for a while. This had been very temporary anyway so that would be okay.

A woman is like a tea bag;
you never know how strong it is
until it's in
hot water.

Eleanor Roosevelt

Chapter 25

I had an arsenal inside a Pagoda to get to, so Jade and I were preparing for me to be gone for a while. I told her the overnight things about Andrew and Zoe, the twins I didn't want to leave behind. I packed a small bag of incidentals from home. The more important items were in the arsenal.

The Bellego House was a mansion owned by a super-rich family. I didn't know how long he would be fighting that fire but had to guess at least overnight, from what I saw when I flipped on the local news. It looked like I'd have to go this one alone without informing him as to the details Jin had relayed after Hammer left. I left a note as to where I'd be and that I had no idea when I'd be back, just that I'd return to our family as soon as possible.

Just before leaving, I got a call on my cell from a familiar number I couldn't quite place. "Hello?"

"Natalie. This is Carl." Okay. Father of Cameron and Courtney. Why would he be calling? We hadn't spoken since they'd fired me.

"Our kids have gone missing," he said. I could hear a lot of emotion behind those words.

"Oh no." Tears formed in my eyes as panic struck me. Although the parents weren't favorite people, I still loved those kids and would never want anything to happen to them. "How can I help?"

"I don't know why I called. Thought you might have a clue, an idea for some reason. It was stupid. Sorry to have bothered you." He hung up.

I paused for a moment, putting it all together, and then raced out the door—which really meant disappeared and reappeared at the pagoda.

When I arrived, Jin and Hunter greeted me. "I got a call from Carl just now," I said. "Shadow Black has their kids. I'm quite certain."

"I saw that you'd gotten a call from him," Jin said. "We have to get you in there," he said. We worked quickly and silently, readying everything for the mission.

He let me know that I didn't have to pack clothes. They would just appear on my person at the right time for whatever job I was doing. I would also have a goodie bag this time like I did on the ship. My challenge, though, was to pack weapons, as I was informed that no hardware outside of what was in said goodie bag would appear for me because of the level of magic in the castle. So I surveyed the situation and packed a large backpack that the smaller one filled with magical items could fit into.

Jin said I had to sleep now, during the day, because I was to go in at night when Shadow Black was sleeping to get a head start on this. I would need the time, as he arose at dawn and started his day of being waited on by his pets. They served him all of his banquets at his royal table in the center of the pagoda inside the castle, but they had to eat in a crowded cafeteria of sorts—total cafeteria food. Disgusting soggy flavorless oatmeal, macaroni and cheese for lunch every day, and tomato soup only. Dinner consisted of salmon and chicken and steak and lavish salads and desserts for him, but crusty old bread and mashed potatoes for them. They were malnourished and weak. Most of the kids were too young to remember any differently, but he could not make them forget their parents, and siblings if they had any. The memories of their families stayed firmly implanted in their brains, until two years in the castle had passed. And then they were wiped clean of any recollection of life before it.

My job was to free the children and disable this horrible entity from stealing any more away from their loving families. There were around one thousand children in the castle, all doing Shadow Black's bidding. If I succeeded, it would create a massive wave of children suddenly showing up on the doorsteps of their families. But I had a lot to do to make this happen. I tossed and turned thinking about it all: the gigantic mission ahead, what I might have forgotten to pack, how exactly I was going to get in, what kind of help I might be getting. I also wondered where Nozomi was here. I could feel her presence. There was a connection, a bond that could not be broken.

Colin appeared, perched near my bed. "Natalie, you must relax and calm the monkey mind," he said, flashing his wide smile. Placing a mug on the night stand, he informed me that this was a relaxation tea made of herbs that would lull me gently to sleep but not keep me there for too long. I sat up in bed and sipped slowly, chatting about who knows what to Colin who patiently listened and responded when necessary.

When I awoke, Colin was gone and nighttime was upon us. I arose quietly, took a quick, refreshing shower and felt fully awake. As soon as I toweled off, the first outfit for the job appeared on my body. I was ready.

~*~

I stood at the window, ready as I'd ever be, preparing to jettison into flight mode so I could survey the castle from above before entering. Nozomi appeared suddenly in the doorway of the still-dark room, looking, from what I could see, healthy and well rested. She was still dressed in pirate garb, but it was clean and unwrinkled.

"Hello, sister," she said, embracing me warmly but quickly. "We are on Pagoda time, and we still have a small window of it to do what I'm here to help you do." A small smile played on her lips.

"I'm so happy to see you, and to see you looking well. What are you here to help me do?"

"We have to retrieve a small treasure chest, about the size of a large jewelry box. I found it a few months back." She had a pirate's accent, and I found it charming and entertaining to listen to but made myself stay focused on the information she was imparting.

"My crew had already started to go sour as a bunch of grapes, so I had to find a suitable place to stash it. I had some mermaids I know and trust hide it underwater so it couldn't be easily found. I believe it's what you need to crack an essential code in your upcoming mission, which Jin has informed me of."

Wow, mermaids? I was glad to hear she trusted them, because if they were anything like the ones in the last Caribbean movie with the scary teeth, I wasn't going there. And wow again, a treasure chest at the bottom of the sea? Really?

"Yes, really," she said, laughing. "It was the only hiding place with enough magic to fake out my crew." She could also read my thoughts. This was great news! We could communicate with no one else listening. Well, almost no one. As if on cue, Jin appeared in the doorway, greeting us.

Nozomi went on to say that the scroll seemed to be in another language, one she had no experience with. "In order to take you to it, I need a ship. The mermaids are guarding it so safely that they won't bring it back to the surface under any circumstances, fearing a pirate trick," she said with a sense of despair. I looked at Jin.

"Yes, we can use *Calliope*," Jin said. I was thrilled, because it meant I'd get to see Charlie again!

"You won't need your arsenal tools just yet, Natalie," Jin assured.

I knew there would be a time when I'd have to go it alone, but for right now this felt just fine, thank you. I was on a mission with those who wanted to help, and those whose help it seemed I truly needed.

Nozomi, can you teleport? I wondered inside my head. She nodded her head. "To the sphere then!" Jin proclaimed. We joined hands and off we went.

We went directly into the sphere without passing "Go" or collecting two hundred dollars or going through the coffee shop this time. Nozomi looked around curiously, taking it all in. I explained to her that this was how we got to *Calliope*, the ship that we rescued her from. We saw the multicolored lights; Jin went first and Nozomi and I followed, shooting out the other side to the lighthouse.

This time, Donovan was outside waiting for us. "Aye, lassies, good to see ya again! Greetings, Jin! *Calliope* is buckled up and ready for this trip. I gave her a tune-up last night so she shines, at least on the inside," he said, letting loose his trademark cackle.

We beamed aboard, and *Calliope* revved up her engine at Donovan's touch. The odd shrink-wrapping of the vessel started and I noticed Nozomi looking curiously at this. Donovan reached into his pocket and pulled out a familiar-looking compass. "Charlie!" I said, helping Nozomi into her seat and strapping in to mine. He floated over to me and plopped onto my knee. I gave him a little squeeze and prepared to descend the depths.

"Hold on, sis!" I said by way of warning. She smiled over at me, and I realized this kind of thing must be easy for her since she still had her sea legs. She looked like she'd be fine. Donovan too.

Charlie, on the other hand, was making some kind of racket! He apparently didn't have sea legs. I steadied him and held him close to my heart. He sighed, which I thought sounded like he felt better. "Th-th-thanks Natalie," he said, shivering.

"Oi, Donovan! Can *Calliope* withstand the deepest depths?" I inquired.

He grinned at me like a Cheshire cat. "Of course!"

We sank deeper and deeper down, and it got darker out the windows and colder inside. *Calliope* slowed down and creaked. Strange sea creatures swam around us, their big bulging eyeballs staring with curiosity into our windows. The farther we descended, the more glow-in-the-dark and alien the fish appeared. I was getting a little creeped out at all of this, hoping we wouldn't run into a giant squid that would try to eat *Calliope*. I wasn't sure how far down they lived, but they were almost as scary as great white sharks, in my book.

"Never fear, Natalie! Almost there!" said Donovan cackling slightly.

With that, we hit bottom with a bumpity bump badump. I wondered if mermaids could actually hang out down here and survive, as it was literally freezing inside our boat now. Icicles were forming around the edges of the cabin.

Nozomi and I unbuckled and stood in unison. Charlie giggled. "You're such twins!"

We laughed along with him, me somewhat nervously as I didn't know the protocol here. How were we to get this treasure chest with the scroll in it, exactly?

"Don't worry, milady," Charlie said, sounding more like a proper Charles at that point. "I am waterproof, and I have a special hydro-flashlight! It's the bomb dig-dig-diggity!"

Well, that was pretty cool, and it solved one problem. As to who was going swimming down here in the deep cold dark with him, that was the question. Nozomi and I looked at each other, similar creeped out. I asked Nozomi if we were in the right spot, and she said we were. The sonar coordinates read it to be so. "No one swims but Charlie!" Donovan announced, and my sister and I sighed in relief.

"Charlie, it's in a circle of rocks approximately twelve feet due east of us, so it won't be a long swim, aye mate?" Nozomi said.

Charlie literally squealed with delight. "Eeeeeeeeeeeeeeeeeeeee! Here I go!" he said. We watched in wonderment as a tiny porthole slid open. No water came in though, and Charlie, as graceful as one doing water ballet, swam out into the dark. Several strange orange and blue neon creatures approached him, but he swam on unscathed.

We saw his little light disappear, and it got very quiet aboard *Calliope*. We waited, not inspired to chat in the cold. After what seemed like forever and a day, we finally saw his light returning, surrounded by bubbles. The magical porthole, which seemed like the only part of the boat not covered with the cellophane-like stuff, opened again, and Charlie came singing right on through! He literally was singing "Eye of the Tiger" by Survivor. I guess he'd been scared after all, but his spirit was valiant and his little heart brave. Impressively, he could also actually carry a tune.

"The chest was a b-b-bit too large to fit through there," he said, gesturing and shivering and shaking the water off of his compass body. "It's r-r-right outside." Apparently he had hitched it to a handle to bring it back.

"Great job!" I said.

Donovan went to the porthole and squatted down to the floor below it. He pressed a button and a section of the side of the boat became glass, like another porthole for viewing, but square. He pressed it again and it slid aside. The water kind of bubbled up and stayed in place instead of rushing into the boat, so I guess Donovan and Charlie had some magic spells of their own going on! He scooted a long pole with a hook outside the window, and grabbed the chest, maneuvering it so it'd fit through this window. At last, he pulled it in!

"You aren't the only one who can finagle some magic, lassie," Donovan said, winking my way. "Now let's strap in and get to the lighthouse so you ladies can open it without being watched." He put the boat in gear to ascend.

In a mass of bubbly propulsion, we ascended and it made us just the slightest bit queasy, but we were fine in a matter of minutes after getting to the lighthouse. Charlie buzzed and danced eagerly around us, but Donovan called him to give us some privacy.

*I'll tell you a tale of the
bottomless blue*

*And it's hey to the starboard,
heave-ho*

*Look out, lad,
a mermaid be waiting for you*

In mysterious fathoms below

**Fathoms Below
The Little Mermaid**

Chapter 26

"What happened down there, Charlie?" I asked.

He sort of giggled and hiccupped and burped all at once. "Well, as I approached the mermaids, they were all in a circle and ushered me in to the middle of it. They spun around me, faster and faster until everything became a blur. And then without a warning the chest was hitched to me, and they pushed me out of the circle so I didn't even have to swim most of the way back! It was fun!" He was positively buzzing with excitement.

The sky had darkened with the passing of the day, and Nozomi and I stood in the very top of the lighthouse, the treasure chest glowing between us. This was the first time I'd gotten a close look at the container, which was not just gold but a combination of layered white, yellow and rose gold, with amber, amethyst and turquoise accents, decorated solely with undersea creatures including mermaids, dolphins, and others.

Looking at it was like looking at a story itself, and as I gazed intently at it, the creatures appeared to be moving! A living story? This was some kind of magic! I had to be careful to keep focus and not get too drawn in. The chest was probably worth millions, and it had obviously had a spell put on it as the seawater had done no damage. No wonder the pirates had held Nozomi hostage!

My sister looked at me intently for a moment before speaking. "Natalie, I'm sorry we lost each other, and even forgot about each other. It seems so unreal that we actually could have forgotten about the childhood years we spent together before being separated. I understand that this was how it had to be for some cosmic reason we can't know right now. But I am so glad to have you back," she said, tears forming in her eyes. I moved over to where she was and hugged her tight.

"The important thing is that we found each other again. You're family, and I love you, sister. I can't wait to hear about your stories and your life, how it's been for you. After we finish this mission, maybe we can have that conversation."

"But for now, we have work to do!" she concluded with a smile.

"Indeed." I waited for her to open the chest, but she didn't.

"I am not sure how. It looks..."

"Hermetically sealed," I finished.

"Yeah," she said. "Hmm..."

We proceeded to both try to pry it open or loosen the latch for the next ten minutes or so, with no luck. I felt anxious. What if we just plain couldn't figure out the opening?

The lighthouse started to rumble. Whoa! Were we having a lighthouse earthquake, here, or what?

"Hold on, gals!" we heard Donovan's voice, from...somewhere. We dove under the table and each grabbed on to one of its legs. This felt very close to a roller coaster I had once ridden at Disneyland called Space Mountain. Rumble, rumble, dip, and slide went the floor beneath us. How safe were lighthouses in seismic events, anyway? Zoiks! Hold on for dear life!

Nozomi and I were literally hanging on to each other with one hand and a table leg each, with the other. We had to ride this out.

And then, as suddenly as this earthquake thingie had arrived, it was gone!

She looked at me. I looked at her. "What was that?" we said in unison. Neither one could muster any kind of answer.

Charlie asked from afar if I was all right, and I said that yes, we were both fine.

Donovan cackled from somewhere below. "Everything's okay here too! We have a visitor!"

We got up and looked out the window and didn't see anything unusual. It wasn't stormy or anything. No boogie monsters or bad guys, no pirates on the sea coming towards us. Nada.

We heard a knock at the door of our room. "Friend or foe?" Nozomi called out with a grin.

"Friend!" said a female voice. I went to look out the peephole, and could not believe my eyes at who was standing there!

And above all,
watch with glittering eyes
the whole world around you because the
greatest secrets are always hidden
in the most unlikely places.

Those who don't believe in magic
will never find it.

Roald Dahl

Chapter 27

I opened the door. "Sam?!"

"Hi!" she breathed, rushing into my arms!

"Hi! What are you doing here?" I could see that she was out of breath from having to walk those stairs. "Sorry about the stairs. I guess it's a lighthouse initiation or something."

"It's okay," she breathed, regaining her composure. "Why, I came to help, of course." She was in head-to-toe silver, a departure form her usual jeans-and-sweatshirt look.

"Nice duds," I noticed. "By the way, let me introduce you. Sam, this is my long-lost sister, the good pirate Nozomi. Nozomi, this is my best friend in the whole world, Sam."

They skipped shaking hands and just hugged. It was like they already knew each other!

"Sam, have you been holding out on me?" I asked. First my cat and now my best friend. How many other people would I be asking this question to?

"Maybe a little," she said, with a mischievous Cheshire cat smile. "But anyway, let's get down to business, shall we?"

She walked and we followed over to the treasure chest. She pointed two silver-polished index fingernails at either end of it, pointed, and shot flames—silver, of course, all round the edges, and broke the seal on this thing in no time flat!

It sort of hissed and then popped open in a cloud of turquoise bluish smoke, or steam or something. "Ahh, that's better. Muah ha ha."

We all looked at each other like, "Did you hear that?" Meanwhile, the voice continued. "Thanks ever so much for opening me. It's been so long, so awfully long. Oh Sam, I owe you one."

Sam studied the chest and laughed. "You're welcome."

"Natalie and Nozomi too," it said. "Oh by the way, my name's Casper." Casper had a low voice that carried at the end of each sentence and sounded rather spooky, but also kind of adorable coming out of a treasure chest. I was halfway tempted to look for some sort of microphone to see if this was rigged! I looked over and Sam and knew she was thinking along the same lines.

Nozomi was more on the same page with Casper, having hidden him in the first place. "I can help you. Firstly though, I need to bestow some gifts." We could see him shuffling through his contents to produce, presumably, the right ones.

Inside there was a bevy of necklaces, bracelets, anklets and large, set jewels themselves, but the contents wasn't in heaps like in most treasure chests from the movies. They were well-organized into rows that looked like a terrace design, and moved in a conveyor belt style one way and then also up in a circular motion to complete a moving wheel. "I like to keep things orderly," Casper the friendly treasure chest whispered, choosing a brooch for Sam that was a smoothed over and polished black amethyst. "This will ground and rejuvenate you, Sam. It will help you break through any emotional blockages. Since you're already so good at breaking the seal on other things, the emotional kind is what you need to work on." Sam smiled and put on the pendant. It let out a barely audible, low pitched hum in the room.

"For you, Nozomi, this green tourmaline and topaz piece." It came up on the rotation and sparkled brightly. Nozomi clasped it around her neck. "This will reconnect you with mother earth, fine tuning that vibration, and will help you learn to be compassionate towards yourself." It was a clear green that looked like the kryptonite in Superman. "The topaz will dispel all levels of enchantment, so if your pirates are in any way still affecting you, that issue will be fixed." The hum of the room increased when she put on her necklace. It sounded a little higher now.

"Natalie…" Casper's voice trailed off. "I have for you…" His innards scrolled through their contents. "Ah! There it is. The Australian Boulder Opal. This type of opal withstands moisture absorption and so it symbolizes staying strong despite circumstances. It's a symbol of hope, and will help you stay focused in times of trial." I picked up the necklace with its pendant of dark to turquoise blues, and placed it around my neck, thanking Casper. The hum in the room increased. The lights in the room went dark and the necklaces started to glow and resonate together with this musical high frequency. It got higher and higher, sounding like a beautiful flute trilogy-turned-solo.

Casper closed and turned a fiery red. "You are now bonded through time and eternity. The power of three is bestowed upon you and will never depart. You will always be there to help one another." Casper appeared to be heating up like volcanic rock. Then with a burst of smoke in the middle of the room, the lights turned back on. Someone laughed, at the drama of it all, I suppose, and the smoke cleared.

Charlie and Donovan were in the room with us, as were Jin, Jade and Hunter. We were all standing in a circle around Casper, who said "Whoa, that was intense! I might be a little charred." Charlie floated over to Casper. "I can help you. He clasped Casper with his handle/hook apparatus and took him out of the room.

"Hi," Jin said. "I'm glad you've all met each other."

There were a lot of mischievous smiles going on.

"Okay, Sam," I said. "'Fess up! How long have you known Jin and Jade?" She glanced at them and Jin nodded her on.

Smiling, she said, "I've known Jin for about a year now. My superpower showed up and then Jin did, shortly thereafter. I needed to know how to deal with it."

"Welcome to my world," I said.

Hunter spoke up. "It's time."

"Time?" I asked.

"Time to defeat Shadow Black," Jin said. I'll meet you at the Pagoda to give you some instruction. Jade must go attend to your children, as Hammer is on the way to another fire."

"Have fun stormin' the castle!" Charlie yelled from somewhere outside the room.

"Thanks Charlie!" I said, nervous laughter escaping my lips. I was hoping I'd have his help but it sounded like I was going in sans my favorite compass.

We all reappeared at the Pagoda. Somehow I had been infused with the knowledge of exactly what I needed, so got busy packing items from my arsenal. I had on a shinobifuku, or secret costume. It was comfortable, allowing for a full range of movement, but it left only my eyes visible to prevent light reflecting off my skin. I wore a utility belt that held climbing gear, shuriken and a host of other fun things.

Nozomi had her own suite of rooms here, and with them, her own arsenal and closet full of clothing. She showed me, and it was mostly pirate attire. This made me think she'd be going back out to sea after she got done helping me with this mission. We had a lot of catching up to do and no time to do it, apparently. Sigh. Maybe someday! I felt like that about a lot of things these days—the family I had created and the family member I had just met: no time.

I didn't have time to follow this thought train, though. There was a job to be done and Ninja Nanny was all set to do it. I'd gotten a message from Jin through our intra-neural brain pattern connectivity waves, i.e. telepathically, that I needed to morale-boost the group.

I gathered my girls. "Nozomi, I know you're ready. Sam, are you ready?"

"Are you kidding me? I live for this shit!"

"Excellent. So here's the deal. After opening the chest…Casper, I mean…we are a trifecta; a triple threat. We are like three pieces that together make up a puzzle. We can't go in guns blazing, though. Your mission, should you choose to accept it, is to help me defeat Shadow Black. He is the fiercest, most cunning ninja alive today, so we have to be crafty. Think like he thinks. We have to be silent, and cunning. I assume that since Jin has trained you, Sam, you have been trained in the art of stealth."

"I have," she said, grinning with a glint in her eye.

I turned to Nozomi. "I haven't," she said looking worried.

"You stick with me then," I said, not at all worried that she'd get in the way. I knew she had to be nimble to exist on the seas for the better part of her life, and that she had a skill set I didn't possess. We were good counterparts for each other in that way.

I had a map of the castle with the pagoda inside, and laid it out on the table. "Remember, Jin said I can't use magic until I get inside. The same goes for you two, too. So that's why all the gear." I handed them each a backpack. "These have what you need to get inside. We will all help each other."

We looked at the map. "I hope to cross at least one of the moats before he realizes we're on his territory. If he realizes it sooner than that, the magic will be stronger, preventing us from getting inside."

When written in Chinese,
the word "crisis" is
composed of two characters.

One represents danger
and the other represents
opportunity.

John F. Kennedy

Chapter 28

Just then, Jin and Hunter appeared. "Natalie. Shadow Black has the twins. We just now found this out."

"Wuh…what?"

"We don't know how or when this could've happened, but it must have been between shifts. Shadow Black is a dark entity, but moves at the speed of light."

"Oh no." I fought back tears. "No."

Jade hugged me, and I held on to her for dear life. "How do I let Hammer know?"

"There's no time. Shadow Black is angry and won't hesitate to try to teach you a lesson with this," Jin said. "You have to go in immediately. You'll be able to fly there. Your magic won't work until you're inside because he has the castle secured on triple levels of anti-magic. He doesn't worry about keeping the innards of the place secured on that level because he doesn't think anyone, including you, will ever be able to get in."

I asked Sam and Nozomi if they were ready, and they nodded. They had already clasped hands with me, so out we beamed into the night sky. I didn't know if they knew how to fly, but they'd said they were ready so I had to assume it was so. And indeed it was. On cold, dark, starry skies we flew and flew until we reached the castle, touching down just outside the entrance of the outermost moat. It was cold, dark and windy. I shivered, so glad to have Sam and Nozomi with me: my long-lost sister, and the person most like a sister but unrelated to me, on the planet.

I didn't know how to cross the moats with the supplies we had, which consisted of a blowup dinghy, very thin wetsuits under our clothes, and that's it, at least for the hydro portion of this venture. The dinghy wouldn't take long to inflate, but on these choppy waters I just wasn't sure it'd do the trick. Too bad I couldn't bring the rowboat here. That wouldn't be fast either but it was sturdy. Swimming in these waters even with our wetsuits on would've meant death by hypothermia, so despite my misgivings I inflated the little boat and we climbed in. It was a wild ride, to be sure. It felt like were white water rafting at times, but we made it across Moat #1 in record time, with all of us paddling.

As we approached the next one the danger of being spotted grew, so we had to stay in stealth mode. The boat was already inflated and the water wasn't as choppy here so that bought us more time. We had to row silently, so I practiced honing my skills in this department, deep in thought about what would ensue once we got inside. There was really no way of knowing, but I suspected he had guards at the four turrets at the very least. I hoped there would be no flying monkeys. As we exited the water I didn't see life of any kind. We ran across to the third and final moat, all cautious as to our surroundings. All quiet.

As I we pushed off for the castle destination, I heard the most godawful sound I had ever laid ears upon. It was a piercing, tortured, low-pitched cry and it was coming from across the moat. I suppose the closest thing I'd ever heard was an orc, like in the Lord of the Rings movies, but this was a little more vicious and sounded more intelligent. Unfortunately, it was answered by a high-pitched something in the water. Anyway, the whole scenario was rather nightmarish and I was really hoping to wake up. I had a sudden urge to just be with Hammer and our kids on a normal day doing routine things.

The thing on land and the things in the water were talking to each other, and I didn't like it. Not one bit. Nozomi and Sam were trying not to freak out, too. I could hear splashing directly behind us. Sam screamed, Nozomi fainted, and I paddled with every ounce of my being.

So here we were in this flimsy rubber contraption meant for a peaceful day at the lake. We couldn't dive in, we couldn't fly here due to our magical powers being blocked—I mean if they weren't before, they certainly were now because our presence had been announced. And, we couldn't very well stand up and fight with our swords, from this boat. There would be no balance and it just wouldn't be pretty. So in essence, we were pretty much screwed. There were horrible beastly creatures ahead, and sea monsters surrounding us, and I hadn't the faintest clue what to do.

I studied these sea monsters for a moment. It was dark, but from what I could glimpse, they were slithery and slimy and had a lot of teeth. I mean a *lot*. If at all possible, I wanted to avoid any sort of contact with these, as I had with the aforementioned mermaids. But the plastic paddle was not a weapon. I was surprised that Shadow Black didn't have anything swimming in or lurking around the first two moats, so I guess there was something to thank my lucky stars for.

Right now, though, these monstrosities were attempting to capsize us. They didn't have arms, so they couldn't really reach up and pull us in, but they could band together and destabilize the boat. Nozomi was still conked out. Sam was still paralyzed with fear. I was still trying to keep my calm face on, but it was just a façade. I was all kinds of freaking out inside.

The pressure from the bottom of the boat started to capsize us. I grabbed Nozomi in one arm and Sam in the other. All I could see were sea monsters, gobbling at the boat. From here, I'm not really sure what happened, because I fainted too, but they tell me it went something like this:

Not every flying hero has a cape.

Michael Jordan

Chapter 29

Out of the water shot our boat like it was atop a geyser! It wasn't a geyser, but a man—a man with arms, abs and an ass of steel. I knew, because I'd met him in California on a road trip with Sam, and he had tried to get with me, but I was in love with Hammer so I passed him up.

His name was Mickey, and here he was. Apparently, he could breathe underwater, and also, apparently, had been assigned to help us storm the castle. So he'd been following us and watching for his opportunity to assist.

We "landed" safely in his arms, or the boat did actually, and he set us down onshore a ways off from the bellowing creatures on land. Nozomi and Sam came to, and as we got our bearings again, we stood to fight as these things as they came at us. What ensued was the nastiest, bloodiest battle I have ever taken part in. Thank goodness for ninja training (yours truly), pirate training (Nozomi), and just plain rage (Sam). Stab! Slice! Sever! Squish! Smash! We ran them through, chopped off their heads, and did every other move imaginable until they were all gone.

Apparently we weren't finished fighting, as the sea creatures then began crawling—or rather oozing, as they had no legs—up the sides of the moat. We had to stab them from above as there were so many (think eels in shape meet Loch Ness Monster in size) and they covered the entire ground, coming at us.

I hadn't a moment to realize that we were now five, fighting together. Marty, Mickey's brother and now Sam's betrothed, had appeared too. We all had swords, and were beginning to wear down. Sam began using her laser fingernails to slice and dice, and somehow managed to finish off the lot of them.

Afterwards, all I wanted was to lie down and sleep, but I had to keep going, and to keep the morale up. I introduced Nozomi to Mickey and Marty.

"We heard you might have…issues to be dealt with, and being the helpful sort, we rushed to your rescue," Marty said. "We're just cool like that."

"And so modest to boot," I ribbed. "Nice to see you, Marty. You being good to my best friend these days?"

"I think she would say so," he grinned, shooting a look at Sam, who flashed her dimples in his direction and then did an almost imperceptible nod in answer to my question. One could see the sparks between them, even in this gloomy, ghastly place.

"Excellent. Now, let's get on with this, shall we?"

With that, we trudged on, forging ahead into the unknown.

~*~

Here we were at the entrance, all five of us. This isn't how I'd imagined it playing out and frankly I was ecstatic to have the extra help. After briefing the boys on the task at hand, I felt confident and ready. Mickey was the eldest of several siblings, and Marty was a younger and slightly more compact version who had followed in his brother's footsteps to become a firefighter. I didn't even know all of what or who we'd encounter here, but I was as ready as I could be. We knew that Shadow Black knew that we were there, so we had to be careful and quick. He had disabled my magic and the powers of Sam and Nozomi, who he knew would be joining me. Since I hadn't known about the others, he didn't either and they could still use whatever powers they had.

The only way in, as far as the eye could see, was up. We had to scale the walls, and we had to look out for each other. As I was getting ready to do this, Mickey and Marty were doing a sort of barely audible "we have one up on these chicks" chuckle. I half-listened until I could take no more, realizing they weren't going to stop until I paid attention.

"What is it already?" I asked, voice overflowing with obvious impatience.

"Well, we..." Mickey started, from behind me. Then Marty took over.

"We were watching your attempt at scaling the castle wall here Natalie, and thought we might be of assistance."

I turned around, slowly. "Do tell."

"How about show?" Mickey said through a grin. With that, he proceeded to put his arm around me, do a medium squat, which I felt compelled to do also, and shoot us up to the top of the castle wall.

"Whoa!" said I, completely taken aback, or atop, as it were.

"Be right back," he said, laughing at my reaction.

A minute or two later, he returned with Sam and Nozomi on either arm. "Special delivery for Natalie Newport," he said, bringing to mind that he had sent me flowers once.

"Thanks for the flowers, Mickey. Sorry if I didn't thank you before. But more importantly, thank you for this. I'm speechless."

"No worries, ma'am. Always willing to help out where needed." He hopped back off of the castle wall, which was really, really high, and popped back up a moment later holding onto Marty.

So Mickey could breathe underwater and jump/fly. I hadn't yet seen Marty do anything, except of course kill critters with the rest of us, which in itself was valuable. I wondered if they both had superpowers.

Marty put his arm around me. "Just you wait and see, Phoenix," he said with a mischievous smile playing across his mouth.

All of this catching up was absolutely wonderful, but I had a seething, growing fear in the pit of my stomach. I had to get to my babies before something awful happened, and free the children this Shadow Black character had imprisoned. I was determined not to let anything stop me on this, the most important mission of my life. Now that he knew we were here, he would move faster in whatever he was planning to do.

Jin's voice sounded like it came from far away inside a tunnel. "You're still on Pagoda time so please don't worry. You don't need to go too fast. Important to be efficient, more important to be careful here," and then it trailed off. I thanked him silently, took a deep breath, and entered the castle at the head of the group.

The child
must know that he
is a miracle,
that since the
beginning of the world
there hasn't been,
and until the end of the world
there will not be,
another child like
him.

Pablo Casals

Chapter 30

The outer castle was cold, damp and grey and though we tried to move silently, our footsteps echoed throughout the halls. It was just a protective shell, I thought, covering the true treasure of the giant pagoda inside. The rain could get inside these walls, but it didn't look like anything else had gotten in for decades, at least. I thought there were going to be sentinels stationed around the outside in the turrets, and there were but they were only statues—a clever optical illusion designed to do what a scarecrow is designed to do.

Sam and Marty were right behind me, and behind them Nozomi and Mickey. I was cautious but felt courageous enough. As in, I wasn't paralyzed with fear.

I had too much training under my belt to fear much of anything at this point. We walked through an arched doorway into the middle of the castle right before the massive pagoda door. I smelled an awful stench and heard a horrible screech, followed by about a hundred more horrible screeches. There were bats in the belfry and they swooped down upon us. As they got closer, we saw that these weren't just any old bats. They were prehistoric-looking, gargantuan bats—as big as we were, in hordes! Gross! They must have been guarding this castle for eons. We all had our swords out and Sam was double duty'ing with her nails. Screech, swipe, screech, swipe, we all went until they were gone. I was drenched in perspiration, looking around to see if we were all okay and it seemed so.

"Well, that was fun," Mickey said. "What's next?"

"You're a trooper," Sam observed.

"Thanks for having my back, everyone. Holy carp," I said, still out of breath.

"Shall we enter?" Nozomi said. It was the first time I'd really heard her speak since we started this. I could see by the look on her face and hear in her tone that she was looking forward to throwing down. She must have had some pent-up rage from her pirate mates turning on her, and I for one highly recommend sword fighting and really, any form of martial arts to get said aggressions out.

We were at the entrance of the pagoda. In a direct circle around it, spanning out about ten feet, everything changed. There were plants and flowers, and butterflies and even fake-painted blue skies with a few sparse clouds on the bottom side of a shade encircling the building. It looked very inviting, in a jungle-like sort of way. At least he had a sense of atmosphere that children would enjoy, I supposed.

I didn't see a way in except the door. The pagoda itself was ornate—carved all the way up the sides with intricate designs and patterns, as if people had spent their whole lifetimes on this project. The vines from some of these plants wove their way up the walls as if they were not overtaking the place, just lightly decorating it. A fountain spilled over into a babbling brook.

Sam tried to laser the door open, but it didn't work. Marty and Mickey tried to use brute force, and that didn't work either. Nozomi and I took our swords to the door, and again, it wasn't giving. So much for any inkling of sneaking up on him, I thought. So I did the only other thing I could think of doing: I knocked.

Almost immediately, the gigantic door swung open and we were greeted by a child dressed all in white, with his face painted like a clown. He bowed low and ushered us inside, not lifting his head again until we were all in front of him. He didn't speak, just motioned us ahead.

I couldn't believe what I was seeing. This whole place was a kids' dream world. There was a pool with waterslides, an ice rink, a merry-go-round, and a miniature version of a whole theme park. There was even a petting zoo. The kids manned their stations, taking tickets, and essentially working the park. They were all the same age, and they all had the same expression on their faces: blank, lifeless stares. It was apparent that they wanted nothing to do with this park. The joy of being kids was completely lost to them, because in fact, most of them were no longer kids. They were young adults or adults trapped in kids' bodies. The whole thing was entirely creepy, and it needed to be stopped.

I gathered that Shadow Black was the one who loved the theme park, and was under some delusion that his automaton "pets" loved it too. I was heartbroken, looking at all the kids whose families had probably given up looking by now. This was a horrible and powerful magic, to cease their growth at this age.

Feeling a hand on my back, I turned and saw Nozomi at my side, tears in her eyes. "Don't worry sister, we will free them all." I didn't hear a pirate accent in her voice at present. All I could hear was a deep inner rage which echoed my own.

I was at a loss. My instincts weren't kicking in and I think this place was blocking any I might've had. Which way should I turn now? How would I find the notorious Mr. Black within this maze? I turned toward the group. "We need to join hands and form a circle," I said. "I need any and all ideas, intuitions, feelings or suggestions thrown into the pot. Don't hold anything back, because it might be the key. Should we let him present himself, or go looking? My Jeet Kune Do training tells me to do the former…to let the energy come at us. But right now I'm just not sure."

We silently formed a circle. All our power combined and I could feel it coursing through my body. It started as a low hum and grew into an audible buzz, and then a shaking. Was this the jolt of our combined powers, or something else? The earth beneath our feet began to rumble and I wondered if Shadow was behind this. We moved to separate corners, beneath decorative pillars the height of tables. I was with Nozomi, and Sam, Mickey and Marty were together. Nothing was breaking except the ground. A hole where we had been standing started to appear, and pieces of flooring started pouring into it.

In a burst of sparks and dust, something came up through the floor and sat itself down directly in the middle of our prior circle. After the debris in the air cleared, I opened my eyes and had a reason to smile: *Calliope*!

~*~

Donovan and Charlie rushed out of *Calliope* in a flurry of excitement. "We made it!" Charlie said.

"I didn't know you were coming! I'm so happy to see you," I replied, giving him a little squeeze. I made a new round of introductions.

"Charlie knew you needed him," Donovan explained.

I heard Sam whisper, "That's so cool!" and giggle.

"Do I ever! How did you locate us?"

"Well," Donovan explained, taking on a professional tone, "we tried to get in via the moats, but it wouldn't work for us. *Calliope* can't jump or fly, but she can ascend and descend and break her way through just about anything, including castle floors."

"She never ceases to amaze," I said. "I'm so glad you're here. Charlie, can you help me locate Shadow Black?"

"Of course, Natalie!" Charlie let out all kinds of beeps, coughing and sputtering while warming up. "He is at the dead center of this building."

I wondered why Shadow Black hadn't presented himself. Determined to get to the bottom of this mess and to decipher the exact character of my opponent, I suggested that we head in that direction. We passed the park area and the décor became very serene and Zenlike. Children overran the place, and didn't react when we passed them by. I supposed that he hadn't trained them to be warriors, as wasn't typically expecting a visit. This was a positive as I didn't know how I'd have disarmed all these children and dealt with all of that while trying to battle my foe.

Up to this point in our so-called storming of the castle, we hadn't been stealthy at all. This could be dangerous. He obviously knew we had arrived, but I wasn't sure if he knew how many of us there were. I did however believe he was waiting until we presented ourselves so he could have the home-court advantage, weave his webs and ensnare us into them. I didn't want to allow this; I wanted to smoke him out of his hidey hole—but since he had my babies, I had to tread carefully into the unknown. Maybe it would be wiser to allow myself into his trap, if that's what he wanted.

We walked down the corridor towards the center of this fortress, and that's when the fun began. The walkway had gotten smaller, so we had to walk single file. A door opened out of the ceiling and a massive ball of legs and eyeballs came at me. It was a giant spider— the one from my dream. The spiders in the movie *Arachnophobia* had nothing on this monster! She was out for blood—mine.

Her exoskeleton-covered body scuttled along the sides of the wall making a loud sound, and I inwardly cringed. I slashed with my sword, but the spider knocked it out of my hand with one of her legs. Trying not to let fear take me over, I did a jump kick and poked one of its eyes with my foot while trying to avoid its mouth and barely succeeding. This only enraged it all the more however, and it lashed out, grabbing me up in its leg. I was very uncomfortably close to its mouth and eyeballs. The spider couldn't plow through the gang and couldn't turn around in the corridor as was too big, so she tried to back up. The claws poked at me and I could hear the spider breathing and see the fangs ready to deliver their venomous bite. This was very much a too-close-for-comfort situation.

"Oh God, I'm gonna die! Sam! A little help?"

Sam was right on it, laser-cutting the legs one by one. Slowly, ever so slowly, the creature fell to the ground. I shivered, sure I'd need counseling after all of this was over, but right now I needed the carcass out of my way. Marty handed me my sword and cut in front of me in our single file line. He opened his mouth and blew, and out came a gale force wind that took the spider's body and anything else that happened to be in that hallway with it! He blew it all the way out of the castle. To where, I don't know, but I never saw that spider again.

"Got lungs?" Mickey said, surveying us and smiling.

Some warriors look fierce,
but are mild.
Some seem timid
but are vicious.

Look beyond appearances;
position yourself for the
advantage.

Deng Ming-Dao

Chapter 31

As we rounded the corner into the main living space, I observed Shadow Black sitting cross-legged, eyes closed, in the middle of a plush, posh, sunken room. The sunken part, three large steps down, was filled with pillows and Turkish carpets. He sat on a pile of folded blankets in the middle of these carpets. Children surrounded him, both sitting with him and, from what it looked like, attending to his every whim. They got him drinks and food, and one of them was bringing him a hot towel for his feet. He lived in the lap of luxury, under some delusion that the kids loved it there or not caring that they didn't. We all looked at each other, equally disgusted and saddened. He had taken hundreds upon hundreds of kids from their homes, and had reduced them to acting like robots, going through the motions of their lives.

The room was encased in glass, or some other clear, hard substance. I tapped on it, then backed up and smashed my sword against it as hard as I could. It didn't budge. Nozomi took a pistol out of her holster, and fired off a few shots—still nothing. Sam tried her laser fingernails, to no success.

I studied my nemesis. He resembled the Pai Mei character from *Kill Bill*. He appeared to be meditating, but then he opened his eyes. They were bright red and he turned his head slowly and stared straight at me. "So, I finally get to meet the famous Ninja Nanny," he said, his voice a high-pitched, crackly cackle that was unbearable to listen to. "So glad you could make it, although I saw that you almost didn't on the way in. Good thing you have such helpful friends. Too bad they can't help you with everything though. *So sad*," he said sarcastically.

I could feel my temperature rising with anger but vowed not to show it or let it get the better of me.

"If you wanted to come in, all you had to do was ask," he said. "But since you tried to force your way in, I don't feel much like welcoming you anymore." He shot lasers out of his eyeballs and drilled a hole in the glasslike wall in front of us. "Sam's not the only one who can slice and dice," he chuckled. "I don't appreciate my pet spider being put to death, especially in such a violent manner. Who is going to eat the flies here nowww?"

He paused for effect. "Helter Skelter, please show Ms. Newport and her friends the way *out*," he snapped, directing one of the disciples sitting at his feet. This little boy turned toward me and I saw his red eyes boring into my very being. He catapulted his body through the hole and came at me at the speed of light, arms and legs punching and flailing.

"That's right, Natalie, I have my little helpers," Shadow Black informed me with an evil laugh.

I didn't want to harm this being that had, I was sure, been innocent before his training, so I ducked as he flew through the air over me and stopped himself just before he crashed into the wall behind us. He was angry now and I was sure that the others were to be unleashed as well.

I knew lassoing the evil demon of this child wouldn't work as rope wouldn't be strong enough to hold him, but he was behind me now so I let the others tag-team him because there was someone else approaching: a little girl with the outfit of Dorothy from *The Wizard of Oz*, but the same red in her eyes. She threw a boomerang at me. It nearly missed my head, chopping off a few locks of hair.

"Oh no you didn't," I said.

"Yes, yes I did. My name is Dorothy, by the way. Nice to *meet* you!" she said in an evil tone as her boomerang returned to her hand. I let her come at me with full force, hoping that she wouldn't injure herself. She had forgone the boomerang after a couple more unsuccessful throws and was doing front flips in my direction.

"Enchanted," I parried, blocking her little body with a simple maneuver, and reaching for a pair of handcuffs that I'd grabbed from the arsenal. I cuffed her quickly. "Another one down," I said, stealing a glance at Shadow Black, who just sat in observance as the next little person ramped up to do its dirty work. As my vision cleared I realized it was two people—a boy and a girl. These worked as a team by holding hands, rising into the air and kicking their way to me.

The kicks were fast and furious, and everything I had would hurt them so as they approached me I stepped aside to let them bypass me. Luckily, they weren't quick enough to detect which way I'd go and Marty was right behind me. He blew them back towards where they'd come from, past Shadow Black and directly onto the opposing clear wall, with such force that they smashed against it and slid down the side. They were likely bruised and knocked unconscious but not otherwise injured.

Shadow sealed off the room after two puppets came hurtling out of it.

Marty's wind gust created such havoc that it blew the arrangement of pillows, tables and everything in the room into a massive tornado! I watched as Shadow Black's belongings swirled around him where he still sat. His eyes burned fiery red and he turned towards me.

"Lest we forget, Natalie, I have possession of two of the most valuable things on the planet of yours," he said. He remained in a sitting position, but rose off of the pillow levitating into the air, and shot like a missile to the outer wall where he literally became a shadow. Scurrying along the wall, giggle-cackling, he zoomed out of sight.

~*~

In answer to his parting words, I thought about how very much I hadn't forgotten that he had my children. I remembered, and was quite nonplussed that we had done the very thing I was trying to avoid—to make him very angry. Now I didn't know where to find him *or* my kids. Just exactly how did one catch a shadow, anyway? This was not going well. I needed to powwow with my peeps, especially Jin, in a major way.

Reading my thoughts, we formed a circle and joined hands. Again I felt the power pulsating through us all. I knew Shadow Black could read my thoughts, so it was pointless to be silent.

"We have to get to him—not necessarily quickly as we are on Pagoda time here, but before he harms my children."

"I believe he wants to make a deal with you," Nozomi spoke up. "I honestly doubt he will harm them before he at least tries to do this deal."

I looked around for other opinions. Mickey and Marty kept silent. Sam nodded her agreement. "I think he didn't just arbitrarily, impulsively steal them. He has a plan somewhere in the back of his crazy and criminal but childlike mind."

Jin's voice came from the center of the circle. "Nozomi and Sam are right. He didn't just take them without thinking about it, and he does want to talk to you, but he wants to lead you on a wild goose chase first. The best thing you can do is to find him. Be careful though: he has set traps to play out this drama. If you fall into them, it will only prolong this process and allow him to laugh at you."

With that, Jin's voice faded and I wondered for a moment what the business was between him and Shadow Black that would not allow Jin to enter here, and only allow him to speak to us for small amounts of time.

We were still in the circle formation, feeling the surge of our mutual powers flow to each individual, all parts strengthening the whole. I think we all had our eyes closed in a moment of mutual harmony at this feeling, unlike anything I'd experienced before.

A voice piped up from the center of the circle, but it wasn't Jin's. "Ms. Newport, missed you I have," said my old friend Yoda. He appeared as a holographic image, much like Princess Leia had appeared in Star Wars.

"Oh Yoda, I've missed you too!" I could feel Sam and Natalie silently shaking with giggles, never having had experienced a Yoda visit.

"Nice to be among you, it is," he continued. "Advice for you I do have. One: find you must, a secret compartment within the private chambers of Shadow Black. Two: open it you must, with this key." Out of the center of the circle popped a tiny silver key that I caught as it shot towards me. "Contains a secret, it does, that will put the fear into your nemesis. Never possessed this key has he, but was told the compartment contains treasures beyond his imagining, so kept it he has, for many years. Read to him what is inside, and if he has any wits at all he will be in agreement with any plans you suggest. Otherwise, to more drastic measures, resort you must.

"Firstly though, distract him you should, so leave his chambers he will," concluded Yoda. I thanked him and heard "A pleasure it always is, Phoenix," before his voice totally faded away.

"Indeed, Master Yoda. Thank you."

I wasn't precisely sure how to cause this distraction, and my confidence in our mission was running a bit low, but I felt that if we forged ahead things would become clear. At least now we knew where in this pagoda-castle Shadow was hiding. We walked on in silence.

Our show doesn't rely on the typical whistles and bells, and smoke and mirrors.

It relies mostly on the music.

Juice Newton

Chapter 32

The children walked mindlessly throughout the amusement park, all empty eyes and painted faces. Some had a simple white paint base but others had clown makeup. This was probably his way of grouping them according to…whatever. They brushed by us like tiny ghosts, not even noticing our presence.

We did our best to scope out the place, memorizing every detail in case anything was to happen. Rounding yet another corner, we entered a little foyer of sorts and I could not believe what our eyes revealed.

Smack dab in the middle of this vestibule stood Sting and Bono. They were chatting in hushed voices. It looked like they were having a heart to heart, and when we entered they looked up and grinned. I think we all did double and triple takes and I was pretty sure we must've looked like cartoon characters at that moment—especially Charlie, who had been silently floating in the air around us for a good little while now, and who said "Z-z-z-z-z-zoom! Vroom! Look who's in this room!" and then did a little spin and turn and steam started coming out of him.

"Hi," I opened. Not brilliant, but it was all I could muster at the moment.

"Cheers, Natalie and friends," Sting said. "We're here for the concert."

"The...concert?"

"Yep," Bono answered. "We were assigned to do a concert in this castle."

"Oh. Wow, okay." Suddenly it clicked in: *They* were the distraction!

Several band members came forward too—not The Police, but other musicians Sting had worked with, and the crew of U2. I thought I heard an excited "dude" from Mickey and Marty's direction, and smiled.

"We file moments like these under 'perks of the job'," I said to my posse. I heard some muffled laughter and knew everyone was still star struck. We didn't really have time for that, though, and so I asked the bands if they knew where they'd be performing.

"We were kind of hoping you could show us," Bono said somewhat shyly.

"We will show you the stage," Mickey said.

"Just so you know, Phoenix," Sting said, "We know why we are here and Shadow Black can't see us until we decide to let him."

"I see. Perfect." This was good to know. Another worry I could scratch off the list. The joy spreading through my veins now was infectious and spread to Nozomi and Sam, who made a comment about having the best job benefits in the world. I hoped she would always feel that way. Nozomi was impressed, but not as susceptible to being star struck as she had always lived on the seas and celebrities didn't hold as much currency there.

"Can you let him see you directly after you're done setting up? Will that be in the next ten to fifteen minutes?" I didn't want us to cross paths with him as he was exiting his chamber, so had to time this right.

"We can make that happen," Sting said. Bono nodded his agreement. I thanked them and all the men headed off to the stage.

"Okay ladies, are we ready to rock this casbah?" I asked, attempting to raise our morale.

"Born ready," they said in unison, with zeal. Oh, how these girls made me giggle. We would enter Shadow Black's chamber and scour it for this secret compartment in relative silence, speaking only when necessary. I wasn't sure if he'd have guards at his door but if so we would disarm them equally as silently.

We heard musical equipment being tested from the stage area, which we had passed in our castle meanderings. Sting and Bono's voices saying "test, test" added an additional unreal element to all of this. They were really going to give a concert here, all in the name of distracting Shadow Black!

"The band members are already done testing their instruments, which are all in order," Mickey said, returning with his brother. "Now they are actually decorating the stage. They brought a big chest with them and when they opened it, curtains, streamers and all kinds of shiny, sparkly things fell out!" Mickey said, his fingers doing a little dance while describing it. This made me wonder for a brief moment about him, as most firefighters I knew didn't get excited about sparkly things. But we could talk about that later.

"They're going to jam first. One test song," Marty concluded. With that, we heard strains of U2's "Desire" starting up. "Oh man, I love this song!" he said, practically chomping at the bit to get back to the stage. I gave him a warning look, not to get off track. "Don't worry, Natalie, I won't," he said, little-boy mopey face showing.

"Maybe they'll film it, too," I said hopefully, and we laughed it off.

As we padded through the corridor, Mickey almost fell into a trap in the floor, seeing it at the last possible moment. "Close call," I whispered. We walked on and on, around corners and through this maze until finally we reached a rickety-looking stairway that was so long it looked like it could lead up into the clouds. We heard the band, a bit more faintly now, giving us the go-ahead that they were about to perform. I looked at the group for a consensus on whether we should all head up the stairs. The two guys said they'd stay down guard the stairs until we got to the top of them safely, and then finish checking the perimeter of the castle for any goodies we had missed, arachnid or otherwise.

The three of us began the long walk, and much to our dismay, some of the stairs also had traps in them to fall into. They were missing the actual step! But after we figured out that there was a method to this madness, we began skipping every fourth stair. So here we were, skipping one stair each and doing a little hop at the end to avoid the fourth stair, all in a line, when suddenly the whole staircase shifted about twenty feet to the left. We struggled to stay planted and heard a shout from far below.

"Are you okay?"

"No!" Nozomi, definitely the slightest of the three of us, had lost her balance and fallen under the railing. She clung onto the stairs, hanging there for dear life.

Sam had slid over the opposite railing and was holding on from the top of that, trying unsuccessfully to swing herself back over or crawl through the railing. Neither attempt was working. I had somehow slid almost all the way off the stairs, under all railings, and was holding on to a stair by the tips of my fingers. We dangled there in space.

We were totally screwed.

"Hellllp!" we all shouted at once.

Mickey bounded up from below, catching Nozomi just as she lost her grip and placing her back on the stairway. He then did the same with the two of us, making us feel light as he swooped us up, saving us just in the nick of time.

"Oh my God. Thank you, Mickey!" I breathed. "I just found you, sister! I'm not going to lose you!" I said, embracing her.

"This place is seriously booby-trapped!" Sam observed astutely.

We felt the stairway start to shift back. Mickey was gone. He and Marty were pushing with all their might, from far below. We heard it click into place again, and resumed our climbing at a faster pace. Starting to fatigue, I slowed down a bit. What was it with these places and their millions of stairs? When we finally reached the top, there were no kids to be seen, just a royal-looking doorway with engraving on it.

As we approached, we saw a light within the floor, coming from below. There were three lights, forming a circle. Thinking this was another of Shadow Black's tricks, we sidestepped, but then noticed that the lights began pulsing, and our necklaces began doing so at the same time. Finally getting the idea of what we were supposed to do, we each stepped onto a light and joined hands.

Out of our mouths came the following words:

"As within, so without.
Always beware and look about.
Under the guise of stormy skies
Rests a calm day if we realize
That with the power of three, we will not fail.
With this power, we shall prevail
Over anything that crosses our path
Solving any puzzle and
Crushing any enemy's wrath
From here may we stand strong
Knowing this is where we belong
Side by side in sisterhood
Working towards the greatest good."

We weren't sure where the words came from, and I think we were too stunned to say much but after they spilled out of us, the pendants on our necklaces burned fiery hot upon our chests, branding us in sisterhood forever. It didn't hurt any more than, say, burning a finger on a curling iron. The lights from the floor disappeared and we were set free to enter the bad guy's boudoir.

His bedroom was plush, just as the sitting room downstairs had been, but with more intricate detail. The theme was completely Asian and all in black and white, with ornately designed screen doors creating room divisions. A huge bed—the only modern thing in the room, which looked like it came from Ikea—sat against one wall and a sliding glass door was open, letting in the night. The curtains were a black and white and beige swirly design and they weren't billowing but flapping ungracefully as the wind blew in from outside. I had to admit, he had impeccable taste. A super-villain with a sense of personal style was interesting.

It seemed there was no one in there but us. We scoured the room for any compartment-type things, finding nothing at all out of the ordinary until we got to the closet. We opened the fully mirrored doors and shoved clothes aside left and right. Nozomi was the one to find it. "Aha!" she proclaimed, running her fingers across the surface of a secret panel in the wood of the back of the closet. Sam and I joined her, pushing the endless wardrobe out of the way to help her. I took the key out of my pocket and handed it to her. They keyhole was so very tiny and she found it quickly; I was impressed with her skills, as we were doing this without a flashlight.

We opened the compartment and all that was inside was a scroll. Sam grabbed it, saying she was the scroll master or something, undid the tie that held it together, and unrolled it slowly and dramatically for effect. She was making me laugh at a time I was completely nervous, and I was so thankful. She even got a giggle out of Nozomi.

"Oh. Well crap." Sam said.

"What?" Nozomi and I asked in unison.

"It's in another language." She handed it over to me. Nozomi and I studied it, not knowing what to make of this. We didn't have a language specialist in the house, and I saw no sign of my kids, so we just took the scroll and silently left the room, for my part relieved that he didn't have any evil slaves lurking under his bed, ready to pounce. It must have been the one room that was off limits to them.

Going back down the stairs was quicker than the ascending had been. It was actually a little bit of a workout, and fun. Sam raced into Marty's arms as she reached the bottom and he swung her around, and Mickey greeted Nozomi and I with a hug.

We could hear the concert going on. I heard the end of U2's "One Tree Hill" and the beginning of "Pride (In the Name of Love)." I was sure they'd have to put on quite the show to keep Shadow Black's attention for any length of time, and I hoped they would so I could find my babies. I couldn't send the others to deliver the scroll as Shadow Black would notice my absence, so we all had to go together, but I wasn't ready yet. I was determined to figure out how to break the spell, free these enslaved children and my own. I felt intuitively that he wouldn't keep my kids too far away from him, so I didn't look too far.

Out of the corner of my eye, I saw the tiniest flash of movement or was it a trick of the light? We were just off of the main hallway, which because of the pagoda's shape, went in a circle. The door to a side room I hadn't seen before was cracked and I went to it and peeked in, seeing a mini jail cell atop a large, raised wooden block. My kids were in it, sound asleep, in little wicker baskets with blankets inside. I clung to the bars staring at them, so peaceful. So happy was I that they weren't being tortured and that no cruelty had been done to their little souls, that I shed a few tears there, in a moment alone. I tried to send a message to Hammer, but my magic couldn't travel that far. I just hoped he felt a vibration on some level.

Everyone else came in, realizing where I'd gone. "Oh my God," someone exclaimed. "Are they okay?" They came rushing to my side.

"Yes." I let go of the bars and let myself be supported by Sam on one side and Nozomi on the other. I might have fainted otherwise. "I can't get to them right now, and I have work to do so I say we leave them here until I've tackled the unfinished business."

I love it when a plan comes together.

Colonel Hannibal Smith
The A-Team

Chapter 33

My nerves had settled somewhat. I began to see the
way to go about things.

"Let's do this," I said, taking charge. "Nozomi, Sam,
I need you to gather the children of the castle. Tell them
Shadow Black wants them to join him in watching the
concert, and that there will be a special presentation at
the end. They need to be there by the time it happens.
Please make sure there is no child left behind."

"Mickey, Marty," I said, turning to them, "please
come with me. We need to set up a trap." Everyone
seemed quite comfortable following my orders—
probably moreso than I was at giving them. Charlie

floated along behind us, still beeping and whirring like R2D2. This must have been his way of taking notes.

We moved quickly and efficiently towards the castle entrance. Donovan was there tinkering with something inside *Calliope*. "Ah, lassie I see that you're ready!" he exclaimed. He finished tinkering, came out and smiled. "*Calliope* is as well, you see! She's been waiting for this moment for quite some time."

We had to allow several minutes for the children to make it to the center stage area. I was so glad everyone else's magic worked here.

"I believe everything is in order with her and you can scoot in and see for yourself," Donovan said.

I climbed aboard and gave him the thumbs up. But I had to find the key to the cage and get my kids to safety. I thought about how Shadow Black thought like a child. He would have hidden the key, and it would be somewhere simple. Simple minds meant simple solutions. Fistpalm.

I went back to the room with Charlie and the boys, and we searched floor to ceiling for anywhere the key might be hidden. Then I felt around the bottom of the cell they were in, and found it taped underneath an edge. Of course! How could I not have figured it out before? So I unlocked the twins, and miraculously they stirred but didn't sleep. Mickey and Marty each carried a basket for me until we got to the stairs, then Mickey squatted and jumped all the way up to the landing—to save time, I suppose, rather than to show off, but either way his skills were quite impressive. He returned for the other twin, jumped up, dropped off and came back.

"Are they awake?" I asked, worried that Shadow Black would detect something somehow if they cried.

"Both were still asleep when I put them down, right outside the bedroom door. His room seemed inappropriate, not to mention windy," he said.

My eyes filled with tears and I thanked him for being thoughtful. I couldn't get weepy now though—no time. I imagined when this was all over, I would become a big pile of mush and emotions, but for now I had to stay strong. What I was very glad of was that on Shadow Black's radar, all of this looked like we were just wandering aimlessly through the place because he couldn't see Donovan, *Calliope*, or Charlie. He might have seen that I found my kids but not that I had unlocked them and placed them somewhere else.

"No problem," Mickey said. "What's all this about, anyway? Why did we have to put them upstairs?"

"Well, we're going to flood the bottom floor of the castle—not all the way but part of it. This is the easiest way to get *Calliope* to the theater area, and to trap Shadow Black. He can't hide in the castle wall forever. He will try to make a deal with me, not realizing I have my kids, and I will play along as much as I have to, to get him where I want him, which is inside *Calliope*. Donovan has been working on a vacuum seal that no one could escape from with any magic. All we have to do is get him inside, and that's that. I don't have to fight him, he just has to die. Once he dies, the spell is broken and the children go free."

I continued, seeing that they understood the plan this far. "You've seen Sam slice; she can also seal. So she has been sealing off the trap doors in the bottom of the castle and any other cracks and crevices that would leak water. Nozomi has set up a pipe that will start adding water from the ocean outside when we give her the go ahead. What we have to do is make sure Shadow Black stays contained and doesn't notice the water filling up the castle, and that the water doesn't get inside where he is in the theater, because we can't have the children come to any harm and because the show must go on until the fat lady sings. Just kidding. It's a lot, I know. Are you with me so far?"

"Are we ever, Ms. Newport," Mickey said with a grin, ever the flirt.

"How will we get to the twins though once the bottom of the castle is flooded?" Marty asked.

"Mickey, can you jump from the top of *Calliope* to the top of the stairs and back? It's risky, but it's the only way I can think of."

"Yes I can. The balance will be off since *Calliope* will be in water. I'll do my best," he said, seeming not doubtful at all but very confident. I headed out to finish this job.

~*~

The castle would take a while to fill with water to the desired level, which was approximately six feet. I went to check on the show and whether or not Shadow Black was losing interest. What I saw on stage told me what I needed to know without even having to see his face.

Sting was just finishing a gorgeous rendition of "Little Wing." Jimi Hendrix was on stage with him, helping him perform! He didn't look like a ghost. He was in full color—purple velvet, of course, or some fabric that resembled it. The only other thing was that he had this golden glow. He might have had that while he was alive, but I never saw him perform then. I was seeing him now. Sam and Nozomi joined me at either elbow.

I knew that Shadow Black was enthralled at this performance, and as a result, completely distracted. One glance in his direction confirmed this: rosy cheeks, childish grin, hands clapping vigorously. Jimi shook hands with Sting and they gave each other a quick hug, and exited the stage. When out of Shadow's line of sight, Jimi looked over at me, winked, blew me a kiss, and disappeared, guitar and all. I caught the kiss and brought it to my heart, sending Jimi a silent wave of gratitude.

I hoped this wasn't the finale as we had more to do. I just wanted to make sure before we set off to do these things, so there I stood in observance, slightly behind Shadow so he couldn't see me or my girls, until the next song started. My wish was granted. I saw that my cats Kiki and Claw were walking a tightrope above the crowd! The tightrope came from where the crowd of children had gathered and ended above the middle of the stage. Shadow Black was so wrapped up in this that he hadn't noticed the kids come in and sit down. He was lost in his own little world of being entertained. He lived for this. I think it was why he had his puppet children attack us instead of fighting me himself. I didn't think he was entirely lazy, and I believed he could fight. In his childlike mind, he would just rather watch a show than be on stage.

"Oh my God, look!" said Sam in a hushed voice, grabbing my arm when she noticed the cats. She and Nozomi gazed upward and grinned. "Your cats are acrobats?"

"I didn't know, I swear," I said. We watched them arrive above the stage, grab on with both of their front paws, and start twirling their whole bodies in opposite directions. The band did a drum roll to accompany this, and the result was so exciting. They released at the same time, both doing triple flips and landing on stage. Everyone clapped. Shadow jumped up and down and around in circles, loving the circus act, still not noticing the kids.

As we walked away, Kiki started to sing. "Six o'clock already, I was just in the middle of a dream…" and I had to smile.

We had to fetch Shadow Black's entourage of evil puppet children while still keeping them restrained so they wouldn't be overtaken by the forthcoming water, so we picked up Mickey and Marty and had them help us. Some of them were still knocked unconscious and some of them were awake and kicked and made muffled sounds through the gags we'd put on their mouths. They were no match for us in their beat up, bedraggled condition, and we carried them one way or another into the room with the cage in it, shoved them all in there and closed the door. I gave the key to Nozomi. We then pushed the cage all the way to the theater and put them just inside, behind where everyone sat. It took all of our combined strength to do this, but it wasn't that far. Sam then sealed off the walls of the room so that no water would leak in.

Arriving at *Calliope*, we reunited with Donovan the Dude and Charlie. "Okay, it's time," I said.

Calliope started up her engines. Nozomi started toward the pipe to start the flooding process. She had planned to get Marty's help with this, because he could use his lung power to make a wind storm and could also breathe in with equal force.

Halfway to the wall, she felt an arm around her shoulder, holding her back and steering her back towards us. The arm belonged to Hammer.

"Excuse me for interrupting, but you won't be needing that. I have a faster way. Hi, Nozomi," he said with a warm smile. "Nice to meet you. I'm Hammer, I'm here to help, and this will be faster than using that pipe," he said, turning my way and flashing me his famous grin. I smiled back, never more surprised as right this moment.

"Didn't know you were a part of this too," I said.

"They wouldn't let me in until it was time. Missed you," he said, dimples flashing and twinkle in his eyes, and he proceeded to put both hands out to either side and fill the place with water. Water was literally coming out of the palms of his hands.

"You all better get going," he forewarned. I ran to him, gave him the most heartfelt kiss I had ever given in all my life, and we all climbed into *Calliope*.

"So your husband can manufacture water," Marty said.

"So I see," I replied, laughing and shaking my head. "I wasn't aware of that until just now." So many things became clear in my mind. He was in high demand in the local fire department—no wonder why.

"You made the right choice," Mickey said, since we had a moment to wait before the water was deep enough to take off. Uh oh, I thought. Awkward.

"Not really awkward, Natalie," he said. "Don't worry. I just wanted to clear the air about that just in case you thought I was here for any other reason than to help."

I honestly hadn't had time to give it a thought, but kept listening. "I thought about you a lot after that trip, and you were exciting and fun and cute and everything, but it turns out I was just missing my on-again, off-again girlfriend and trying to fill a void, as we were in a long distance relationship," he said, searching my face for confirmation that I understood. "The flowers I sent you were a sort of 'nice to meet you' gift as opposed to a 'let's see each other again' one.

"Believe me, I so completely understand," I said. "Thank you for explaining, I appreciate that. So…are you on now, then? She was pretty. I met her at the restaurant she worked at."

"Wait, you *what*?" he said.

"I know, right? It was total happenstance, although I'm not sure I believe in that concept anymore. We stopped to eat on our way home, and she was selling the calendar you were in, so I felt like a bad person, having slept in the same bed with you even though nothing happened." (Nothing really meant *almost* nothing, as he had kissed me but we had stopped at that).

"Wow," he said, a bit stunned.

"Yeah," I agreed. "I didn't show Sam right then. She got the calendar I bought for Christmas."

"I can vouch for that," Sam said. "She totally held out on me. Never, ever, *ever* do that again," she said, straight faced, and then burst out laughing. "I thought she was carsick."

Marty shook his head. "The tangled webs we weave," he ribbed, punching his brother in the arm. Mickey punched him back. They were both in good spirits though. We didn't have time for any of their brotherly roughhousing, so I hoped they wouldn't start that.

"There's no room in here anyway, Natalie," Mickey said. "And to answer your question, yes, we're together," he said. "Happily for over year now."

"That's wonderful," I said with utmost sincerity. "I hope I get to meet her someday. Err—*re*-meet her."

"I'm pretty sure you will," he said, a mysterious smile playing upon his lips. Perhaps he knew something I didn't. Perhaps he knew the future. I just wasn't sure what anyone could do these days. My own husband was a superhero, and I hadn't even known it until now.

*It's important to remember
that we all have
magic inside us.*

J.K. Rowling

Chapter 34

The castle was filled with water, and we were all aboard *Calliope*, outside the theater. Nozomi had left a small space at the top of the room on one side for *Calliope* to get in using ropes and pulleys that the guys had set up. Charlie connected us to them, and we were hoisted up with the help of my old friend Vin Diesel, who had arrived at the last minute as well. He basically teleported to inside the theater after getting an urgent message from Jin that we needed an extra pair of hands—and strong arms, and…well, I could go on but I'd just get distracted. I still had a bit of a thing for him and probably always would. It couldn't be helped.

It was just as well that it happened this way, because Hammer had to leave. "Babe, I've got the kids," he said, and somehow or other, he did have them and was going to be busy babysitting them at home unless he got called to a fire. In which case, Jin and/or Jade would take over.

I sat on top of *Calliope*, and finally Shadow Black could see me. Everything that was happening on stage sort of dissolved. The performers either had gone backstage or back where they belonged. Shadow saw that somehow I had gained the upper hand, looking at the flooded castle, and it angered him.

"Natalie, I offer the following proposal," he said, sounding more grown up and reasonable than I had heard from him so far. "I give you your kids back, and you let me wipe out your memory of this place and it will be like none of this ever happened." I guess he still didn't realize I had discovered and freed my kids.

"That's a nice offer," I said. "However, I offer you the following compromise. You free these children and agree to be a good ninja wizard. I know you never wanted to rip them away from their families and their lives, or rejoice every time you saw a missing child poster. I know you never meant them any harm, and you never meant to turn any of them into evildoers either."

To this he just laughed. "Oh Natalie, how naïve you are," he said. "I want things my way. I want to live in luxury as I have for so long now. I can't do that without keeping them. It's not like I haven't provided them with

places to play," he said, dragging out the last syllable of
the last word, as usual.

"Okay. I wanted to give you one last chance," I said.
"Since you're not taking it, I'll just let you know that I
already have my children and they are out of your
possession. Also, I like to keep my memories intact,
thank you very much. It just helps me deal with life, to
store as much knowledge as possible up in here," I said,
pointing to my noggin.

His face got white for a brief moment, during which
I saw his transparency. He had no legs to stand on now
and he knew it. He could disappear, but where to? His
home was flooded, and he didn't know that the upstairs
hadn't been tampered with, and whatever magic we
could use inside this castle, was all being used upon him.

"I have a scroll that was meant for you," I offered,
reaching out to him, and then put it in the crook of
Charlie's handle so that he could reach it.

Sam was sitting inside *Calliope* and was fine.
Donovan, Mickey and Marty were keeping her
company. Charlie was with me. Shadow Black's eyes lit
up like a kid with a Kit Kat being dangled in front of
him, and he got up and reached out for the scroll. At
that moment, Mickey and Marty each grabbed one of
his arms and pulled him inside, where he was restrained
in a special chair created just for this moment of this
day. Donovan, who I hadn't known could do this,
disabled Shadow Black's magic with a spell, and sealed
the deal by sprinkling some Charlie dust on him. It

actually looked more like Charlie had spit on him, which was rather hilarious and got a few laughs.

I handed him the scroll. The least I could do was to see what his reaction would be, since he had been led to believe it contained the key to all the riches he would ever need in the world. He unrolled it and gave an exasperated groan. "What does it say?" I asked.

"It says, in an ancient Japanese language, 'All you need is love; love is all you need.'" With that, he crumpled up the scroll and began to do this horrible combination of snarling and crying, and we sealed the doors to *Calliope* and used the pulley system to go back up the wall and through the hole to the water side.

Before being lowered to the water, I looked back at all the children, whose faces no longer had the horrible paint on them. They were all remembering each other and from their expressions, they were overjoyed. They looked up at me and said a thank you to all of us in unison. One by one, they began to disappear from the theater, no doubt being cocooned before being returned to their homes. I made sure Cameron and Courtney were among them—and they were. They had been his last capture, so they had barely had time to be initiated and brainwashed. They were the only kids who saw me in the group, and I locked eyes with each one before mouthing the words "I love you" to both. Then, they disappeared, being returned to their parents, who I was sure had learned a lesson and would appreciate and value them much more now.

Shadow Black's spell had been broken at last. The evil ones also had been set free and looked completely fine now—no red eyes, no scary teeth, just healthy looking kids.

Through the water, Sam unsealed a few small sections of what she had sealed up before. "Hopefully, Hammer won't get dehydrated if I don't give this back," she quipped. The water drained out quickly and we all exited the belly of *Calliope*, leaving the villain restrained inside, and formed a circle. Jin's voice came through the middle, right before he appeared there, smiling. Since Shadow Black's spell had been broken Jin was apparently able to come here now. "A job well done, Natalie, Nozomi, Sam, Mickey, Marty, Charlie and Donovan," he praised. "And Hammer, though right at this moment, he is at home now with the children. He will be back shortly with the kids and their necessities."

"Thank you for your help, Jin and Jade, and Yoda, Sting, Bono and company, and Vin, again," I said. "I never could have done this without you."

"You are welcome." With that, Jade appeared as well, and gave us each hugs—I loved that we had graduated from the Japanese tradition of bowing to this.

Please join me back in the theater," Jin requested.

We all walked there and again, for about the billionth time in the past few days, our eyes widened and our jaws dropped. The space had been completely transformed into a Kabuki style theater! We were invited to sit down and watch, as Jin and Jade reenacted the whole story of their birth and their lives all the way up to this point. They did this fairly quickly, knowing we were all tired, but this was actually dinner theater, as we were served a delicious bento box meal by waitresses in kimonos. I'd no idea where they, or the other actors in the play, had come from, but I realized I'd really worked up an appetite. Somewhere in the show, Hammer had snuck in. He had the kids in brand new strollers, and they were happy to see their mommy. I introduced Nozomi, who I could tell was going to love being an aunt.

I now understood why they had needed me to defeat Shadow Black and couldn't do so themselves. Shadow Black had killed Jin and Jade's parents, and put a spell on Jin and Jade, preventing them from retaliating. He had been a friend of the family as they had grown up, and was in love with their mother. When she chose another he couldn't handle the rejection his true love gave to him, and seethed with envy, so evil took him over and he murdered them both and then decided to take revenge on them by enslaving as many children as he could. Jin and Jade had both gotten married and had kids, who had been inside this castle for years. They hadn't gotten a chance to know their kids as they were growing up, as they'd been snatched by Shadow Black as babies. Jin and Jade were always so happy to babysit and now I realized why.

"What will happen to Shadow Black?" I asked.

"Much the same as with the pirates gone bad, *Calliope* will take him into the ocean where he will be...disposed of and recycled within its depths. As you know, the ocean cleanses everything. It is your element," he said, reminding me of the time we were in Hawaii and he'd told me this, which now seemed so very long ago.

Jin and Jade's own children were the only ones who had stayed behind to meet their parents. They had two children each—four and five years old. They had reunited tearfully and joyfully and soon the toddlers were playing together quietly, as if none of this had ever happened.

Jin and Jade asked us to come up on stage. One by one, each of us was honored with a medal for our valiant efforts and service to their cause. I was the last one to be recognized. "Natalie," Jin said. "Little Phoenix. Thank you so much for everything you have done in the name of saving the children of the world and our own children. I'm so sorry that your children were taken in the process. That wasn't meant to happen. Luckily, you have an open-minded husband who was ready to step in when I called upon him." I noted that Hammer was back and looking on, from the audience, a twin in each arm.

"You should know, I have been training him for the better part of a year in martial arts, so you are not the only ninja in the family," Jin said.

This got laughs from all of our friends. I shot a look at Hammer, as if to say "really?" and he nodded, smiling like I had never seen him smile. He mouthed the words "I am so proud of you. I love you," and I just about melted right there on the spot. Jin bowed to me and then hugged me and presented me with a medal around my neck.

It's a good thing I didn't melt though, because I felt something on my back—or, rather, in my back. It was wings. I had grown wings. They were taking me up, and up, and up into the sky. I could feel the wings supporting me. They were so strong. I looked down and saw everyone looking up at me in surprise, and then saw the castle from on high, and it was in flames and had been reduced to ash. This is all I could see.

I was so high up—I could see the stars like they were very, very close and all at once I was no longer flying, but had landed on something, a sort of suspended light grey platform, in the middle of the night sky. Surprisingly, it wasn't cold up here. I was pondering the miracle of the universe and "how it's all connected," as Sting wrote, when he himself appeared, sitting next to me on the platform. He nodded a greeting.

Since he was the one who had given me advice on how to fly, I wasn't too surprised, all in all, that he was the one to show up, or summon me here, or whatever. I was again dressed in a white sparkly bodysuit, which matched my white, sparkly wings. Our legs hung off the edge into the nothingness, and I thanked him for helping and for doing a special concert just for the occasion. "Oh, quite all right, Natalie, it was enchanting," he said.

I laughed and asked him what he was planning to do now that this was all over. "I'm going to go on vacation, and then maybe go on tour," he said.

"Oh good! I've seen you in concert several times in the past—but never like today," I said.

"I just wanted to tell you that you were right, you are a phoenix. Your life is some of the greatest poetry I've ever experienced," he said. "I will be writing a song for you. Co-writing, actually. Bono and I actually spoke about it."

At this point I think all my dreams had come true. This was a dreamy collaboration and one that could mean a lot symbolically for the world as well. "Oh my," said I. Just then, Hunter appeared, floating up from underneath us, out of the darkness, as stealthy and silent as ever.

"Natalie, I wanted to take this time to say thank you, as I'm not allowed to reveal my identity to everyone in the castle. On behalf of Jin and Jade: you have honored their families and brought them back together. Truly, no one else could have done it."

"I had help," I said, reflecting back at him.

"That you did. But you were instrumental in this mission, and that deserves my deepest respect." He bowed to me. "Just so you know, all the coffee shops I own contain portals like the one you have used. So...whenever you need."

"Thank you, Hunter." He paused before continuing. "You are a phoenix, arisen from the ashes of your past. The fire you saw below was an instant blaze and cleansed everything, as fire does if it is allowed to fully burn."

Though I knew it would make him feel uncomfortable, I hugged him anyway. He looked at me for a full five seconds or so, smiled, and then turned and flew away, his cape fluttering in the surprisingly warm wind. Sting was still there beside me, a small smile on his lips.

"Come on, we must return to the castle," he said, putting his arm around me in a friendly gesture and pulling me off this little platform and into the night.

I have a feeling that my
boat has struck,
down there in the depths,
against a great thing.

And nothing happens!

Nothing…Silence…Waves.

Nothing happens?
Or has everything happened,

And we are standing now,
quietly, in the
new life?

Juan Ramon Jimenez

Chapter 35

We landed outside the entrance, taking a long look at the castle. What before had been dilapidated ruin was now transformed. The fire I saw hadn't been a fire at all, but the flash of everything being renovated, and I felt that everyone inside was fine, just fine. I took a deep breath and steadied myself, gaining control of my emotions before walking inside.

Hammer met me. "There you are. Have I ever got something to show you," he said. I glanced behind me to see if the wings were gone, and they were, but I was still wearing the same sparkly outfit.

Walking through the castle, it was no longer just a cement frame but a fully decked out castle with all the trimmings! Chandeliers, fancy furniture and décor adorned the entrance and everything beyond. It was literally fit for a king.

All of the interior furniture and decor that had been there, plus Shadow Black's theme park, had disappeared and been replaced with every kind of luxurious goodness I could imagine. The pagoda now had a fountain in the middle where the theater had been, and a full Zen garden and all the modern amenities inside— a movie room, pool and ping pong tables, and a hot tub. It was childproofed and at the same time totally gorgeous. The wall hangings were some that had come from our house, and I saw the Feng Shui décor we had chosen all around.

Jin joined us. "My dear Phoenix. You didn't know this, but by finding the scroll, you undid all of the mischievous and more serious spells that Shadow Black did through the years, and you actually set love itself free.

You have done the hard work, and the medal was a symbol of that but this is your real reward. You defeated my arch nemesis, so you inherit the castle and everything within," he said. I looked around in awe. "You and your family can live here for as long as you wish. If forever is your wish, then so be it," he concluded.

I thought for a moment, and looked at my husband, knowing he would agree with what I was about to say. "Jin, would you and Jade and your families like to live here with us? I mean, it's an awfully big castle for just four," I said, winking at Hammer, who nodded in a way that told me this was exactly what he thought I should do.

"Since you asked...we would love to," Jin said, motioning to Jade to join us from wherever she had been hiding.

Jade finished his sentence for him. "We would love to, Natalie," she said. "Anyone you want to live here can live here."

"My sister..." I trailed off.

"I think Nozomi will be returning to the high seas," Jin said. She just feels most at home there. But perhaps this could be her port in the storm." I smiled at the thought of that.

"Where is she?"

"She returned to the Pagoda to prepare for a mission."

"I see, I see," I said. "And Sam?"

"Sam is watching your kids, who are upstairs. She is with Marty."

"Mickey?"

"He returned to California to his job and his girlfriend." I was sorry I hadn't gotten a chance to thank him and say goodbye.

"Like we said, you can ask anyone to live here that you want. There are ten bedrooms." Ten bedrooms!

"Hmmm." I looked at Hammer. He nodded. We could all live here. We went upstairs to ask Sam and Marty, first. "Hi guys," I said casually. "How would you like to live here with us?"

Sam blinked, shocked at the thought of it. "Whoa-do you own this place?"

"We do now," I grinned.

"With 'us'?" she asked.

"All of us: Jin, Jade, their kids, us and our kids, Nozomi, and Mickey and his girlfriend if they are interested."

Marty smiled. "A band of misfit superheroes?" he asked, amused.

Sam swatted him on the arm. "You mean the coolest superheroes ever, of course," she said, correcting him.

"Why, sure."

"How about Donovan and Charlie?" I was sort of thinking aloud now, knowing that they had gone back to the lighthouse. Maybe the lighthouse wasn't so far away from here. I was pretty sure I could visit and ask them later.

We'd all be leaving our jobs, but that was okay. You see, we had new jobs. I would be working to save people from fires. Hammer and I would be partners in this. He could still work for the fire department if he wanted, and I could do whatever for employment. But neither of us would have to. The castle came fully stocked. It was a magic castle, and food was provided with it. Food enough for all of us. The rest of the crew would be able to help with these kinds of crimes and disasters too, and we would all be able to fully relax when we got home to the castle

"Natalie, you should know that we all have superhero names now," Mickey said, grinning from ear to ear.

"Is that so?" I said, returning his smile.

"Yeah, that's so. You can call me Surge," he said.

"I'm Windstorm," Marty said.

"Slice," Sam said, pointing her laser nail at the air and miming that she was slicing something.

"As long as you call me Ninja Nanny, or Phoenix, I'm totally good with that," I said. "What about Nozomi?"

"I guess that remains to be seen…" said Sam, trailing off.

Everything was coming together perfectly, so much so that it felt dreamlike.

I just wanted to know one thing. "Jin?" I summoned softly.

"Yes, Natalie," he answered. This time though his answer wasn't coming from afar but from just downstairs.

"Can Yoda stop by and maybe crash here once in a while if he is tired and needs a rest?"

Jin laughed—the second belly laugh I had ever heard him do. "Of course, Natalie. Of course."

Oh great ocean,
oh great sea.
Run to the ocean,
run to the sea.

U2
One Tree Hill

Epilogue

The next morning, I awoke from a very sound slumber, the first in years. I rolled over and Hammer was beside me. I looked around the room and for a minute I forgot where I was, and then remembered everything. The kids were beside us in their crib. My beautiful babies, Andrew Makai and Zoe Mer, had returned to me and were unharmed. How would their future be different from now on? I really had no idea, but I felt big things were in store for them. I wanted to kiss their little faces but didn't want to wake them—or Hammer for that matter. Everyone had been through a lot, so they deserved to sleep in.

Feeling I'd gotten enough of a slumber to be functional, I slipped out of bed, heading downstairs on

what was now a carpeted and not-creepy-at-all staircase.
My cats sat in the sunken living room that now had the
fountain in it, and a skylight. I padded down the stairs
and greeted them, picking them both up and kissing
their furry heads and putting them back down.

"Well. I never knew I had such talented kitties," I
said. "I knew you were, but never just how much."
Since I was awake, I didn't expect them to reply.

"Nnnnnnnatalie. We've been waiting for you down
hererrrrow," said Kiki.

Okay, so after all the times I had tried to get them to
talk to me while awake, they were finally speaking.
Nothing shocked me these days, since they could not
only talk but sing and do acrobatics. "Sorry to keep you
waiting. Yesterday was pretty tiring."

"Yesss. We know."

"I can't thank you enough for your acrobatic
dexterity and your musical prowess. You kept the show
going when I was sure Shadow Black was going to lose
interest and come looking for me."

"You're welcommmmme," they said in unison. "We
recognize that your life issss full. We thank you for
every minute of time you've sssssspent with ussss." They
were still speaking in unison now. "We love you,
Nnnnatalie."

"I love you too."

Just then, the strangest thing happened. They both stared at me and started to glow. Their bodies glowed gold and their eyes turned the most beautiful shade of purple I'd ever seen, like deep amethyst.

"We've been with you to help, but were only designed for this purpose on earth. There was nothing by chance in you choosing us; in fact, we chose you, because we knew our mission was tied to yours." I noticed that their kitty accents had left them and they spoke to me as humans would do. "Since you have much to accomplish, we are moving on to fulfill our own destinies in the afterworld. Thank you for honoring us."

I honestly had no clue what to say. Being sort of stunned speechless, I muttered a thank you in return, and I think I told them I loved them again.

"We love you too, Natalie. We will still visit you in your dreams," they said.

"So long and thanks for all the fish," they said, smiling at me one last time. I swear those were their final words to me, and it made me laugh a little. They had both always been such characters.

With that, they solidified into statues the style of King Tut, raised up off the floor and floated backwards until they meshed into the wall behind them, into two spots that I hadn't noticed before, their exact shape and size. They sort of clicked into place, and *Kiki* and *Claw* were in typeset beneath them.

"Oh, my," I said. I had to admit, this was a lot better than having them pass away, but they were my furbabies and I would still miss them terribly. Touching both statues, I said my goodbyes and shuffled out to the castle entrance still full of emotion. Though I knew logically that this would give me more time with my kids and that made me happy, I wasn't ready to say goodbye to Kiki and Claw yet.

The three moats had gone and were replaced by only the open ocean, and a two lane road leading up to the castle. All I could see for miles was water and that road, and I gazed out towards the sea. A few boats dotted the horizon, but one larger vessel seemed to be getting closer.

As I live and breathe, I said to myself. It was Nozomi's ship! Somehow, she had gotten it back, set sail and found the castle. I stood up and started to wave. I saw her waving back from the bow of the boat. Hammer joined me at my side, and kissed me good morning. "Are we going to have guests?" he asked groggily.

"It's Nozomi," I said giving him a huge smile.

"Oh, that's wonderful," he replied, and left to go get showered. I knew he wanted to hear about her life and what she remembered of our childhood, as did I.

Spotting a place she could moor up, I ran to it and directed her there. When she arrived she tied her ship to it and said "Ahoy there, sister!" to me. She seemed very cheerful as she hopped off and came to hug me good morning. "No more moats?" she asked.

"No more moats, and a lot more modern amenities," I replied, ushering her inside. It was a bit chilly out and the cold sea air was starting to seep into my bones, as I was still in my pajamas.

"Whoa!" she exclaimed upon seeing the remodeled castle. "I'm impressed!"

"Thanks, though I had nothing at all to do with it," I said. "It happened while I was flying in the sky last night," I said, and she laughed with understanding.

"I saw the whole thing," she said. "I was allowed to view what happened after I left so I could understand everything."

"Don't you just love the pagoda? I mean, the place itself and how time sort of stops, and how they really are forward thinking."

"Yes! I've never experienced anything like the pagoda. It feels very modern and very ancient, all at once."

"Exactly," I said, offering her coffee and breakfast.

"That'd be lovely, thanks," she said. While I stumbled around the kitchen I was not yet used to, she helped and listened as I asked if she wanted to live with us. She paused and looked at me thoughtfully. "Thank you so much for the offer, my beautiful sister," she said. "But my home is and always will be on the high seas. I just can't be fully myself on land, no matter how hard I try. I will however need a place to anchor down on occasion," she said, "and hope it will be all right with you if I stop by from time to time."

"I totally understand about the land legs versus sea legs, and yes, of course you can visit anytime. I wouldn't have it any other way."

"Thank you. In those cases you would be seeing me in the morning as I'd sleep on the ship but come in to visit during mornings or evenings, or just whenever convenient for you. I wouldn't want to intrude," she said.

"Don't worry about that. I've invited the rest of the gang to live here as well, actually. There is so much space. We could all go *days* without seeing each other."

She laughed, acknowledging this as she looked around. "Also…" she paused, considering how to frame her next phrase. "I might be needing your help with a mission of sorts," she said, speaking softly, but quickly so it all came out at once.

"And what mission might this be?" I asked, smiling and intrigued.

"It's my husband. The pirates on my ship, they took him. I need to make sure he's not in Davy Jones' Locker," she concluded, tears forming in her big, dark brown eyes.

"Oh, no! I didn't know you had a husband. They took him?"

"Yes, when this started and they first began to go sour and corrupt," she said. "They said they'd return him when I handed over the treasure, but there was never any treasure to be handed over, so they just never gave him back."

"You can't find him anywhere?"

"No. There is no trace. It's easy to do, on the high seas. So much can be hidden there, and the laws are so nebulous that most times they're not even obeyed. Most of the pirates I've ever known have been lying, cheating scoundrels," she said.

"Nozomi, I'd be happy to help," I said, still tired from the last adventure but ready for the next one too. "The others can assist, I'm sure."

"Thank you, my sweet sister. I am lost without him," she said, the tears finally overflowing from her eyes onto the table. Somehow her crying made me cry too. I think I needed a release from all that had happened. As we sat there blubbering, Sam came in, with tousled hair and eyes half open.

"Hey, what's with all the tears? You inherited a castle-pagoda. This is supposed to be a happy occasion. What gives?" she asked. We laughed through our tears.

"Hello sleepyhead," I said.

"We were having a good sisterly cry," I tried to explain. "But it looks like Nozomi here could use some help," she said.

"Really," she said more than asked, in a most interested tone. *Do tell.*

Right about then, my own hungry husband sauntered in to the kitchen, fresh from the shower. Nozomi wiped away her tears, saying something about allergies. "What'd I miss?" Hammer inquired. "Not breakfast, I hope!" I heard his stomach growl and stifled a giggle.

"Don't worry, you didn't miss a thing. Just some girl talk," I said, winking at Sam and Nozomi. "We'll continue this conversation later," I said giving them a sly smile.

Hammer didn't pick up on it. He was already nose-diving into the refrigerator, going for the orange juice. Sam had turned on the baby monitor, which Hammer had brought with him when he returned, and I could hear the kids stirring awake. I felt lucky that they slept as long as they did. I guess Hammer only had time to grab the essentials. I guess he could teleport with kids in tow.

And I guess I had a few things to talk to him about—
what was the extent of his superpowers? Would he
always teleport to work, and how far was this place
from anywhere we were familiar with, anyway? How
would we entertain guests here if they couldn't teleport,
and didn't we owe his co-worker a dinner
party/barbecue? Would we be keeping our smaller
house to keep up appearances?

"Natalie, calm yourself. You should know by now
that we can *all* hear your thoughts," Jin said, appearing
at the sliding glass doorway and startling the bacon out
of my hands and onto the floor. I laughed, and everyone
joined in. We were all in good spirits, and even Nozomi
seemed temporarily distracted by the goings-on.

"Still sneaking up on me! Knock that off already!
Want some breakfast?" I was determined to add
"hostess with the mostest" to my list of
accomplishments, but first, Natalie needed a nice, long
nap. ☺

293

Dear Readers:

I hope you enjoyed the sequel to *Ninja Nanny*. It was a labor of love, and again I used National Novel Writing Month (www.nanowrimo.org) as my launch pad. I carried this story inside me for a few years before finally having time to let it out. If you're one of the readers who has been patiently waiting to see what happens next, since the first version especially, thank you for your patience! I'll do my best not to have it be so long until I write the next one. Life does ebb and flow as far as opportunities to write, though, so there are no guarantees. I'll try (she said, Yoda's quote "Do or do not; there is no try" echoing in her mind).

I'd love to know what you think so please feel free to review this book on Amazon, Goodreads, or wherever you review books normally, especially if you loved it. ☺ Also please like my Facebook page and follow me on Twitter to keep getting updates. My website is www.natalienewport.com. Check it out! I believe we all have some of Natalie in us, some of Sam and of Nozomi. Which do you relate to and why? The same could be said of Hammer, Mickey, and Marty. Which would you choose, and why?

Thanks for sending *Ninja Nanny* some love. 10% of the proceeds will go to Seacology (www.seacology.org).

Stay strong,

Ninja Nanny

Coming Soon:

The fog didn't clear at all as we drifted through a small bay in Nozomi's ship—the same ship that her pirate crew had taken over and imprisoned her upon. We had both thought the ship was lost and gone forever, destroyed by a triple sea tornado, but as it turns out, the vessel did not in fact suffer the same fate as the pirates aboard it.

"Yer ship is good as new," Donovan had announced, presenting it to Nozomi after all was said and done at the castle.

"Thank you!" she squealed with delight, climbing aboard to survey any possible damage, and check for what was left aboard. "I'm home again!"

"You are indeed, lass," Donovan said. "You might find a few things missing, but only the loose items that would've blown away in the storm. Everything possible has been retrieved and repaired, including your beautiful ship herself," he finished.

"You *fixed my ship*?" she asked, eyes wide.

"With some help from Charlie," he replied, eyes sparkling. With that, Nozomi ran to embrace Donovan, thanking him profusely, and asked where Charlie was so she could thank him as well.

"He's at the beach with Casper. They're getting along famously," Donovan said with his signature chortle.

She headed out to find the unlikely pair of friends before setting sail again, to say goodbye and thank them. They had gotten really attached during the castle-storming adventures. "Charlie! Charlie, where are you? Casper?" She walked along the sand, seeing nothing and no one but miles of beach and water. A few steps later, she saw the tracks of a box that had been dragged out into the water. Wading out into the shallow, she couldn't see anything but tiny rocks and shells. She ran for the span of a mile in either direction, not finding Charlie or Casper. Returning to the lighthouse, she reported that she believed Charlie and Casper had gone missing.

After an unfruitful search of the lighthouse, thinking they might just be playing in some secret hiding place, Donovan immediately called out a search party of all his seafaring friends.

~ * ~

Nozomi and I sailed her ship together in silence, both thinking about the sweet little compass and the treasure chest, inanimate objects that had come to life and helped us in the first mission we had completed together, along with Sam, Mickey, Marty and Hammer. We suspected that they might have disappeared to the same place Nozomi's husband had disappeared to, but weren't sure who was behind it.

We had been at sea for nearly a week. My babies were back at the castle where we now all lived—the whole group, except Nozomi who lived aboard her sailboat. Hammer was watching them, and Sam would watch them when he couldn't. Jin and Jade had their kids help watch mine, too, so that all worked out.

Our current mission of looking for Nozomi's long lost husband was interrupted, or added to, by the search for Casper and Charlie. We scoured all of the ports we could find within a certain radius, looking for clues, anything suspicious. We had asked at every port as well. Sometimes our questions were met with suspicion, and other times genuine concern, but we had yet to find anyone seeming to be covering something up.

Nozomi had brought her cat, Fluffernutter, who was very much a seafaring fellow. He could sniff out danger, too, as well as critters and dishonest, scheming pirates.

"He does this thing when he encounters a human he doesn't trust. He will lie down and put his paws over his eyes. No joke," Nozomi had said. I hadn't seen this cuteness yet but it would mean we were in the company of scoundrels, so it'd be a good clue.

We continued to move slowly through the fog until we reached the edge of the bay, listening for motor boats and any other sounds that could be a danger. Then at last, we reached the edge of the fog bank, and it totally cleared up! The sun was out although there was still a chill in the air. I could see why Nozomi liked the open seas. It felt so peaceful out here. Until, of course, it didn't.

Calliope, Donovan's boat, approached us, and we were happy to see it, and him, thinking maybe he and his mates had found Charlie and Casper. We saw Donovan come up top, and...what was that look on his face?

His brows were furrowed, and I had never seen him looking that way before. Was he worried about the lost ones, or was it something else?

A few minutes later, I no longer had any doubt what was causing the look. A flash of silver at Donovan's neck told me everything I needed to know. "Ahoy there, lasses," he said. "Do you think you could help an old feller out?"

A crystal skull shined aboard Calliope as the boat drifted through sunlight and shadow. We watched in horror as one by one, Nozomi's old crew appeared. Every one of the evil pirates we thought had perished in a sea storm and turned into fish food, down in Davy Jones' locker, was aboard Calliope. One of them held Casper, and another held Charlie, and each had a sword in their other hand. The pirate at the front, I had never seen before. He was dressed all in black with a blood red scarf around his waist, his eyes were sunken black holes of horror, and he had a malicious grin full of yellow teeth on his ghastly white face, underneath a pointy grey beard with barnacles in it. For a moment, he looked familiar, and I gasped with shock to realize that I was seeing Shadow Black's ghost, with a very real knife at Donovan's throat.

"We meet again, Natalie, and Nozomi. Two for the price of one," Shadow Black cackled. "It looks like you have a few things that belong to me, starting with that sailing ship you're on," he said, the holes where his eyes had been scrunching up into slits as he smiled cruelly, pulling the knife tighter to Donovan's throat.

About the Author

Between penning novels, Natalie Newport enjoys unraveling the secrets of the universe. She does so in her gym and in bookstore cafes, mostly, and occasionally at concerts, in nature, or on the open road. She lives in Arizona.

www.ingramcontent.com/pod-product-compliance
Lightning Source LLC
Chambersburg PA
CBHW070830250626
47159CB00003B/723